# COOL FOR YOU

### EILEEN MYLES

a novel

# Cool for You
# Eileen Myles

**Soft Skull Press**
**2000**

COOL FOR YOU
by Eileen Myles
© 2000 Eileen Myles
Published Fall, 2000
Soft Skull Press, Inc.

THE AUTHOR *would like to acknowledge the following journals, anthologies and web sites which published excerpts from this book:*

*Transience and Sentimentality,* (The Institute of Contemporary Art, Boston, Ma), *5 x 5 singles, Fence, Murmur, Queer 13, Less is More, Boston School catalogue* (ICA, Boston), *Provincetown Arts, Fetish,* and *Blithe House Quarterly: a site for gay short fiction* (www.blithe.com/) and *Nerve.com.*

THE AUTHOR would also like to thank Helen Marden, The MacDowell Colony, Blue Mountain Center, Hide & Seek (The Bucknell Art Gallery) and Stuart Horodner, the former Soviet Union and Persephone Miele, Ryszard & Maria Wasko at the Artist Museum in Lodz, Poland, Kathe Izzo, Michael Carroll and The Schoolhouse Art Center in Provincetown MA and Provincetown Arts and Jennifer Liese, Elaine Showalter and Annie Iobst, Stephanie Grant, Maggie Paley and Jane DeLynn, Lia Gangitano, Kathleen Finneran and Joe Westmoreland, Bill Sullivan, Jennie Portnof and Matthew Stadler, Marylyn Donahue, Joan Larkin, Tom Carey and Robert Harms, Mary Rattray, Ann Rower, Myra Mniewski and Rumi, Peggy Griffin and her mom, Michelle Tea, Sara Seinberg, Marcie Blackman, Sini Anderson, Sash Sunday and all the girls and boys of Sister Spit, Louise Quayle, Sander Hicks of the brave and visionary Soft Skull Press, and especially my great love, Karin Cook.

EDITORIAL WORK on this book was done by Lenni Wolff and Sander Hicks. The interior was designed by David Janik, and the cover by Scott Idleman, for Blink! Design. It was published in the year 2000 by Soft Skull Press, Inc., Vanguard Publishers of the Lower East Side. Please feel free to visit us at www.softskull.com.

COVER PHOTO: "Rocky" (1983) by Jack Pierson.
AUTHOR PHOTO also by Jack Pierson.

PRINTED IN CANADA at Kromar Printing LTD., Winnipeg, Manitoba

SOFT SKULL PRESS, INC.
*Vanguard Publishers of the Lower East Side*
100 Suffolk Street
New York City, 10002

*For interactive information on this title and others of similar high quality and daring, please see our situation on the world wide web, www.softskullcom.*

*Jamais real, toujours vrai.*

—*Antonin Artaud*

*for Nellie Riordan Myles*

# North Building

# 1.

I've made up a myth in my life that any time you push yourself through something uncomfortable, say a snowstorm and you don't have boots on, then you will get the job, because you have been so doggedly good or so stupid—you knew just when to push on. Like most things I pretend to believe it's usually not true. My feet are wet and I've got nothing (like right now) but of course once things happened that way and it wasn't really all that wonderful. It's how I got my job at the Fernald School.

I was driving a cab in Cambridge. I know I've told you this before but I'm lonely tonight and it's raining out. The cab was yellow of course and it operated, I mean it got customers by one of those radios, a little pick up thing that this guy's scratchy voice came out of and because I was a girl and a fuck-up I didn't get much work. Some guy stopped me in Harvard Square. Ran up and said, can you take me to work. Where do you work. He looked like a hippy. The Walter E. Fernald School. It's in Waltham. Show me okay. Sure…it's right up on Trapelo Road.

*Trapelo Road.* It was one of those Italian-sounding names my mother always said. Trapelo Road, she'd go to Aunt Anne on the phone and now I was having my own relationship to the streets of the world. It was snowing hard. What do you do there?

The following Monday I was climbing up the hill that led into the place. I was trying so hard not to lose my mind. Later I was trying not to lose it in San Francisco. Maybe the problem was I was always drinking so much, but it felt like everything.

This is the place where you find out if your head is screwed on tight enough, said Tom. He was the Director of North Building. I was thinking he had a really little head, a pretty little head and then he was opening the door to a room full of them. "Severely retarded adult males" was the classification. He said there was a book called Pandemonium in Crisis about the place. There used to be a bunch of ministers from Cambridge who did all the jobs instead of college kids like us and the legend was the ministers would fuck them and kill them, the residents. We didn't call them patients we called them residents. It was this funny kind of school.

Outside the building next to mine was a porch and it overlooked a green hill and a lot of trees and a young guy sat out there with his legs crossed and he was rocking slightly forward again and again. It seemed like he was in rhythm with every little thing there was. I'd walk in each morning, onto the grounds of the school, and see him swaying and feel incredibly sad that he could exist like that and I could not, and then everything that was inside....

Do you know what it's like to smell a building that's full of shit? Human shit. It was like dying and going to hell. It was just like that every morning. Hardly awake, hungover and the darkness of the barely lit walls and the distant groans and shouts and laughter and the smell of human shit in the walls. And disinfectant. It was like it fixed it a little bit and then it got worse. It was like clouds in the stink.

Tom flung open the door like a real sadist. Peter was coming toward me. Skinny head, big lips. In a way they all reminded me of boys I knew in grade school. In kindergarten. I mean if they grew up absolutely the way they were. Will you play with me. Gonna have a party, gonna have cake, something like that. Feet kept coming my way. Slow. It seemed like one in front of the other like baby steps. Another guy down on the floor, baggy pants around his hips. Da-da, Da-da. There was something intensely erotic about this guy. His whole being felt like drive and it was perched there, demanding Da-da. His hair was black. He looked like Napoleon. There was a wondrous, wondrous boy named Bobby Doyle. His eyes were blue and ecstatic. He was my diaper boy, a beautiful baby. His eyes were whirling around. He walked on the balls of his feet and he looked like a beautiful centaur. His hands were outstretched and dripping down his fingers like a kangaroo. And he was immensely, immensely happy.

The one who said Da-da, I remember, was pissing a lot. His dick was often out and he would piss right on the floor. The name of the job was nurse's attendant. We made about a hundred dollars a week, not much. We were all recent college graduates and most of us wore earth shoes and the guys had pony tails. I wore boat shoes. Things are different now, said Tom and part of the difference was that as well as the book, there had also been a famous movie, Titicut Follies, about Massachusetts institutions, and so the local caring community, mostly emanating in this case from Harvard, had decided that Fernald would be an excellent target for a behavior mod program.

I was delighted to be inside an institution and not because I was nuts. My father's mother, Nellie Myles, had spent the last seventeen years of her life at Westborough State Hospital. My parents would never let me go in when we visited her. They would just make faces because it was so horrible. I was lucky I was five they insisted because they in their thirties did not want to go inside. It's interesting to think of my parents as such young people with the obligations of having two small children and a mentally ill parent, or one perhaps just interned for a very long time. They said Nellie's hands were clenched tight for years. I had always wanted to go "inside." Inside anything, so Fernald would do.

At Harvard they had devised this wonderful program and Tom told me this was what I would learn. Each one of these men had some form of negative behavior we didn't like. Bobby Doyle, the glowing centaur, generally had no clothes on. Nakedness was his negative behavior. The man who went Da-da kept pulling his dick out.

Actually his pants were too big so they were slipping down as well. He was a little guy, short, with excellent sharp features. He had passion. There was a tall character named Francis who also couldn't keep it in. He had a huge nose, was probably in his mid-forties. You would walk in and go, Hi Francis how are you doing today. He would look at you moistly, going, Today, Today. You'd go, Cut it out. And he'd look right back laughing at you, going, Cut it out, Cut it out. It was the greatest joke and you felt he was the sane man in here and you were one of the fools. He had a condition called echolalia where he would simply repeat the last thing you said. It was disturbing to see how little I required of a conversation, how easily duped I was into believing I was heard. Francis had snot pouring out of his nose and there was usually a gleam of it striping the front of his shirt. I have pictures of these guys I took on my last day at the school and I thought of them as my children walking around in the sun. I left there in the Spring.

We had these meetings at the Shriver Center. That was the shiny facility at the front of the grounds where politicians and scientists would visit to see how things were doing at the school. No one ever came back to the residences and even the Harvard psychiatrists who designed the programs rarely did and then it was with undisguised expressions of disgust. It was disgusting. The place and the smell and these guys. At the Shriver Center we would discuss each boy's bad behavior—the nudity and exhibitionism. I don't think there was really much else. Swearing. There was an old man, Walter, who was really schizophrenic and he would loiter over by a big window in the corner holding his massively outsized trousers like the folds of a dhoti, and he would murmur and mumble fuck you Leroy goddamn piece of shit, bitch crack up your ass. Go to hell.

One of the things you learned quickly about the Fernald School or

North Building was that it was a nightmare of misclassification or just no classification. Walter should have been in a mental hospital, not a state school for the mentally retarded. But of course, seeing this place, what's the difference. His problem was he swore. And we had a chart. Each one of us nurse's attendants. Usually we were two on a shift though there would be long expanses of time alone either because of someone's days off, or they were needed elsewhere—or, as the social relationships among the attendants became more complicated, because somebody wanted to fuck with your head.

This guy, Mark, my partner, who I will tell you more about later, had the theory that if they had IQs of 40 and mine was really great—150 or 172, then it would just sort of average out, and they would get a little smarter having one of us around but their stupidity would be overwhelming. Alone with them you became an idiot. Half your intelligence, it was clear, arose from congress with other people. Or something from them. Here you got nothing. So alone, dumber and dumber you'd go.

Up at the Shriver Center we were given our tools. The chart for each guy on which the day was broken up into fifteen minute intervals. And we were given aprons to wear, the kind newsboys use. Attached to our aprons were little time pieces that went off buzzing every fifteen minutes. In the aprons were band-aid boxes full of chocolate stars. Once back in the locked wards of North Building we would hear the buzz and quickly scan the room to see if any penises were exposed. If Bobby Doyle was naked. If he were clothed I would go up and hug him and say, "Good boy, Bobby!" And I would give him a chocolate star. This was very good for me. I would feel swept up with a feeling of beneficence when I was administering hugs. I wasn't that kind of person, who went around hugging all the time. This was the early seventies when it seemed that everyone wanted to give you a nice back rub which quickly turned into a sexual opportunity. I just couldn't see letting anyone who rubbed my back fuck me so I didn't get touched much. I liked being the dispenser of positive emotion in a population that wouldn't identify me as a slut. I was tired and now I had a job.

The psychiatrists at Fernald would teach us these methods and then when we did our reinforcements correctly they'd go, "Good work, Eileen!" I cringed at that for the obvious reasons—being totally uncomfortable with these "good parents." It was a middle-class thing to get stroked for doing a good job. Where I come from, the confused upwardly mobile working class, such encouragement was slimey and manipulative. You were supposed to do a good job and if you didn't you would get fired. There was something rotten about this slippery in-between where the assumption was they could get more from you by patting you like a dog. They were right. It was embarrassingly true.

My partner Mark and I took up the reinforcement therapy with a vengeance. We wanted to quit smoking. We wanted to be good. All around us was the subtle feeling of a campaign for self-improvement. If we were daily, moment by moment, improving these men's capacity to live "normally" then what could the therapy do for paragons of intelligence like ourselves. When the buzzer went off we would hug each other for not smoking. Because naturally behind the closed doors of the ward we could do whatever we wanted. It was a smoker's job. Probably it was a drug addict's job. One day Mark gave me some speed and it was a terrific day at work and the guys made tremendous progress. In these freedom-loving times we were being handed something scarily wonderful. A discipline.

Of course helping these guys advance our sense of their autonomy was a wonderful thing. But the psychiatrists at Harvard were not so much older than us. Some of us (there was this married couple, for instance, who were going to graduate school) had incrementally improving lives but mostly I think the other nurse's attendants fell into the blur of "Cambridge people." The slightly educated well-meaning down-and-out confused.

Our lives were a mess and we needed training too. Mark and I became fast friends through the many hours of internment we shared. Things never got very intense in the ward when there were two of us.

Everyone seemed to know their places and we would entertain each other with stories about our lives though I can't remember a thing about this guy except he wore earth shoes, had gone to college in Vermont. Had a beard and long hair and my initial impression of him was evil. He invited me to his "house" for dinner and then it got weird. I never understood what men wanted from me. I mean I always knew but the unfamiliarity and the predictability shocked me again and again. Why would you want to fuck someone you didn't know. Perhaps I was spectacularly good looking. I don't think so. I was just female and relatively young. Very young, 22. Mark was maybe 26. He had already been around too long. He shared his house in Somerville with several "people." Boys, girls, who knows. There was an animal smell to the place, old furniture. These kind of lousy tossed-down lives. He made dinner and we brought it up to his bedroom. It was probably some rice thing. He was probably macro. He started rubbing my back. It felt weird. He was speaking in this soft voice he had never used before. Maybe a little bit with the residents when he was trying to get them to do something. (Which we weren't supposed to do. Behavior modification was about freedom). He persisted for a while, asking me if I wanted to hear some music and holding my hand and looking into my eyes. All his behavior seemed patently geared to hanging in until I got the picture that we were going to have sex. I was almost missing that that was his intent, it felt so vague and meaningless. Finally I said I had to go. I was sick of sitting in his room. By now he had retreated to petting the cat and speaking with her. He looked up smiling gently with flashing anger in his eyes. You know, it's going to be weird with us now, he said as I went out the door. It really felt like a threat.

Mornings I'd stumble into the storage room once I'd waded through the stink. We started work at seven. I was usually late. In the storage room I'd grab an apron which contained yesterday's band-aid box and flip the lid and fill it full of M&Ms. The chocolate star phase had passed really fast. We were doling out teeny little orange and yellow and red and butterscotch M&Ms. They were cheaper and you could really buy them in bulk. And quickly they got hard as a rock. There was a huge cardboard box full of them in the metal cabinet in the storage room. I dipped in with my band-aid box and then I'd often grab a pawful and pour them in my mouth. That was a bad day. I could tell I was fucked instantly—pouring hard old M&Ms down my throat at 7:15 or 7:20 usually meant it was all over already. Because I'd be dipping in all day, not really capable of eating human food and there was something frightening about being completely plugged into what we were reinforcing them with. I was gorging on the prize and I was dizzy.

I've had a funny association all my life with work and candy. Nuns were my primary teachers growing up and they all had big food problems. In fifth grade we had the candy nun, the one who supplied it and stored it for the whole school, and candy was a big money maker at St. Agnes. Sometimes during a math test Sister Jenilda would tell us with an extra element of angry fear in her voice that no one, no one was to turn around. And then you'd hear her creaking the wooden cabinets open at the back of the room and the soft but unmistakable rattling of candy papers and the quiet murmur of her satisfied chewing. We'd all be smirking and giggling wildly and we would make a silent chorus of chewing pig faces at the front of the room that we could slyly appreciate in giggling profile. Oh grade school how I miss you!

After school when I was fifteen I'd take the bus down Mass. Ave to the Harvard Coop where I rang the register for a long time at the candy counter. It's where I gained twenty pounds. I'd slam a Lindt hazelnut bar down on the floor and then feel compelled to eat it because it was broken. I thought hazelnuts were the most ethereal taste in the world, almost like a whistle! That milk chocolate just began melting, rather than being brought there by body heat like the processed chocolates of America.

The M&Ms numbed me. I went reeling out into the dark red halls and my first responsibility was to make sure everyone was out of bed. It was a treacherous feat because inevitably there'd be a few stragglers: big James and his smaller friend guiltily rolling around with shit encrusting their long nailed fingertips. It probably felt good, it was sweaty and hot and dark and I, in the grip of my chocolate jones, was spoiling it. I'd pull the blankets off them and rustle them up, guiding them in the direction of the clothes room where we would dig up some duds. No one's clothes fit and that was the look. I think they were all donations and in my thrift shop mentality I also went scouring through the endless racks and bags for a sweater or two for myself though like the M&Ms there was something creepy about taking their goods. But of course I did.

I'd often see Mark in the hall, actually right away after our episode, and he would give me a manic look and dash upstairs or be thoroughly engaged in talking seriously with the married couple and they'd all give me a bored nod that radiated loser. It seemed to me that he had probably told them after I would not be his girlfriend that I was a bad worker, not serious or concerned or some kind of fuck-up. And he was absolutely right the only thing was that he was a fuck-up too but now he was playing good and I was the pathetic outsider.

Sometimes when I would see him dashing by in the dim halls, particularly in the early morning when I had a hangover, I would think that his penis was a devil's tail, you know like it had an arrow at the end, it was forked. And that would utterly scare me and freak me out but mainly I was glad I hadn't fucked him because a sight like that would put me right over the top and I really didn't want to go. I mean I knew it wasn't true but it was just like this emotional tattoo I put on him that summed it all up, scared me and left me alone. Like I said, I went to Catholic schools and it had not so much marked me for life as marked life itself with funny, holy and evil pictures. I was scared then, and I'm still scared now, but I'm flashing these pictures to you.

I couldn't work and Mark couldn't work either but so what. I had never had a job so far in my life, a failed working life of already eight years and longer if you counted baby-sitting. I somehow did everything wrong: dropped things, daydreamed, forgot what they said, and would get insanely angry when I was tired and be rude to the public. Also I stole. I wanted more than I earned and usually you were surrounded by people who were richer than you like at the Harvard Coop and it seemed I should have a little more. At least to buy records.

I remember a girl named Kelly Parrot (Puh'-row) and she had gone to Beaver Country Day School if you can imagine such a name and girls like her worked at the Coop too and everyone thought it was a good thing that she should have a little job. Taking a little time off from college. Daddy would come in and his hair was parted down the middle and he loved his daughter and he was an alum. All these people had a certain colored skin, kind of golden peachy and expensive. It was leisure skin, I thought and slammed another Lindt on the floor. I was getting pimples and they were not. There was a day when all the alums would come back and crowd Harvard Square and wear fake straw hats which had class of '39 on them etc. and everyone was so happy and sometimes they had a young golden son with them, and even outside you could hear the goony Harvard Band marching around the Square and when you rode along Memorial Drive they would be out there sculling and you could see it was their river and you were entirely fucked. Slam.

# 2.

What my family had taught me was to not know how to work. I was
not allowed to touch things, I had no idea how things worked, and I
was not forced to clean my room. I didn't have to do homework. My
mother would occasionally ask but I would lie and that was okay. My
parents did not want us to be like them and it was true. We would
probably be even less. We couldn't even work. We were too fucked-
up. My father hated his job, and now he was dead. He had been a mailman. My mother kind of liked typing, but people made her nuts. She
would imitate them at dinner. She was their secretary and they could-
n't even spell. She could. Every word in the world except "myrrh" and
that's how she lost the spelling bee.

I won mine—I tied with this other girl. For my prize I got a plastic
cross with one of those outdoor roofs. You know the ones I mean? It's
very American. If you go to a park in the country, a national park,
you'll see weather info on a brown wood sign with a small protective
roof. Picture the sign in plastic, still brown, about five inches tall with
a neon Jesus on it. Jesus has to absorb light to glow.

The girl I tied with was a tall red-head from a lovely family and she
later went to Marymount—one of the expensive Catholic girl colleges.
Her name was Dana and she was quiet and calm, kind of bowlegged
and she always looked like she wanted to say something—her eyes

would blink like she had just been distracted from her purpose. I loved her dark red hair. I thought she was beautiful and I wonder what she would have said.

One evening, half my life ago, I was standing at work. I think I was a hostess at the Fenway Motor Inn in Cambridge. I was wearing this two-piece check maxi suit—it was in the 70s. I was watching boats go down the river. The window in front of me was like a page and I was writing in a spiral notebook and I got this idea: I drew a sad woman's face and I wrote what she was thinking and I thought, why can't I be famous right now. Why can't I just act that way. Why can't I record everything down like my life counts, like I'm the Queen of England or Bobby Vee, and that way I can be safe and not have to wait to die to be important. Why can't I live right now. Because I am not rich, I am not a saint. But I do know this: not all of us were sent here to work.

Dana's best friend was named Judy, she was a doctor's daughter and it was clear they were both stinking rich. The nuns acted differently towards them. Just the way the nuns pronounced their last names suggested they were vassals to these families' greatness. So much was expected of them. They arrived at St. Agnes with the understanding that they would be friends. It was a neighborhood thing. They came from the rich neighborhood, and those kids took the bus to school together. I mean I had friends in my neighborhood too, that was normal, but I also knew it wasn't important to my mother that I stick with them. I think she was kind of hoping I'd get away.

Everybody wanted Dana and Judy to be together. And they were so different. Judy was wild and a little hysterical but she wouldn't just do it like the rest of us. I mean, be bad. They were all like that, the girls from Morningside. They'd have their one big night and then they wouldn't talk to you in school. It was a femme thing. So they broke Judy. Because she wanted to have fun. You could see it happen. She was in the cemetery drinking beers and waving bras with the rest of us one night, shrieking, and then she was gone. It was like maybe she left school for a while, got really depressed. All the rich girls' parents would worry about them and send them to therapists. I'm so screwed up, they'd wail. Pathetic. Cause then the kid would wind up convinced.

# 3.

For this was I born, for this came I into the world? I was in the bathroom mopping up shit. Bobby Doyle's I think. You're familiar, I suppose, with these disappointed words of Christ. Was he hanging on the cross when he began to whine? Florence Nightingale once wrote: "Christ, if he had been a woman, might have been nothing but a great complainer."

I, Eileen Myles, twenty-two years old, mopping up the huge turds of a beautiful young autistic boy—I only wondered sadly if I shouldn't be someplace else. I thought of the mean little faces of the young Harvard shrinks who had given me tools to lead these men to freedom. If they were still fucking up, I was fucking up. Once Bobby started peeing on the floor right in front of me—because of me it seemed—and I went to stop him and he fell down on the floor, laughing, and protectively held himself in a fetal curl and my boat shoe raised to kick the little prick I hated him so much and I freeze that moment in a picture and I hand it to you: my failure and my shame.

I've often thought of a female Christ. David told me there's one in a church in Montreal. Mostly the world can't take it. Because of people's feelings about the delicacy of women and also because of what a meaningless display female suffering simply is. If you belittle us in school, treat us like slaves at home and finally, if you get a woman alone in bed just tell her she's all wrong, no matter what sex you are...or maybe you just grab one on the street and fuck her real fast—in an alley, or in her own bed.

I mean if that's the way it usually goes for this girl what would be the point in seeing her half nude and nailed up? Where's the contradiction? Could that drive the culture for 2,000 years? No way. Female suffering must be hidden, or nothing can work. It's a man's world and a girl on a cross would be like seeing a dead animal in a trap. We like to eat them, or see them stuffed, we even like to wear them, but watch them suffer? Hear them wail? The complaining lines were expunged from Florence Nightingale's book.

I identified with Bobby Doyle. He was lily-white and radiant. His eyes were dazzling blue like my one true boyfriend in college, Mike, who had excellent dreamer eyes. Bobby's eyes were totally unsoft. Blue could be fire, could be dynamic, icy, explosive and forbidding. Bobby was a fortress of solitude. Always laughing. What he liked to do was take all his clothes off and get down on the cool bathroom tiles and curl up against the frost white porcelain of the toilet. It was his mother and he was her little animal. He would cuddle and rub his cheek fondly against her again and again. I knew how it felt. Don't you? Nights when you're drunk and the whole world seems so unbelievably distant and you lay flat under the powerful overhead light in the ladies room or at your friend's apartment and it is the only safe place in the world.

Bobby made little clicking sounds, little snickering birdlike gusts of laughter. I was like him but they broke me. I didn't want to be here. I was a little glowing bird who heard hundreds of sounds and was swaddled by streams of color and light and they made me wake and listen and come out and be here and go to school and I was in hell, no matter what happened. I wanted to kick him in his eggshell sweetness. I wanted to see his yolk flow.

I remember the first day I went to school. I'm sure I was alone. A large fence surrounded the big brick school and there were many children, there were endless puddles and nuns. It was a grey day and I felt a need to exhibit my bravery. I had heard of school and this was it. I gulped in some air and made a big chest. I became Perry Como, Mario Lanza, and sailed into the schoolyard singing my heart out. It was as if I was the wind, a storm and all the other children were dull phenomena. How can they stand it, I wondered—my power?

A nun eventually came over and asked me my name. Eileen Myles, I told her. She looked at me seriously. It seemed like enough. Yet after that, daily, I was more and more under their sway. Bobby Doyle was free. He would snatch a single strand from the broom and jam it under his fingernail and start spinning and spinning. Usually on one foot, which had huge arches so the ball of his foot was almost a hoof. He walked on tippy toe. It was the manner of his dance. Around and around looking at the piece of straw as if it were the center of the universe and he, a medieval philosopher, was giddily staring into the heart of the mystery.

Also he liked to eat cigarette butts. There was a debate among the attendants whether to let Bobby have them or not. We all knew we could modify his behavior better with an old stubbed out Tareyton than any fucking piece of candy. Even the psychiatrists were unsure. Finally at one of our meetings one shrieked, of course you can't let him eat cigarette butts as if it were the obvious answer to a moral question. We knew he was as confused as we were. Are cigarette butts bad for you. Are they bad for Bobby Doyle. What was he made of? Something triumphant I think.

# 4.

One day alone in the ward I decided to put on a show. I come from a musical family. I'm named after this operetta, Eileen. It's totally unknown outside my family. The heroine on its album cover is a gorgeous brunette who is standing on a precipice in her Irish shawl. Her lover down below is shouting up. I wanted to be him, the singing man. I wanted his clothes. The right to serenade, rather than hanging out in such a rough spot—on a cliff in a storm, being adored.

The part of Mark's message I missed when we stood in the locked ward not smoking, and hugging each other every fifteen minutes, was that I needed him for my sanity. It was scary in there alone. Because it wasn't just my intelligence I felt slipping away in North Building. My whole life had become a big mental health experiment. The one ploy I possessed, other than to do absolutely nothing, was to cast sanity to the breeze when in doubt. So up, up I went, stepping from arm to arm of the red and green imitation leather chairs, one day after lunch, around 1:30 or two.

The boys were feeling nappy and full. They were installed in these chairs and some were snoring and some of them drooled. Generally if I sat in a chair I felt like one of them. Which was something I couldn't do. I began to sing. I started at the chair nearest the southern window. *Oh-oklahoma when the wind comes whistling down the plains. Dah-dah-doo-doo-dah-dah doo doo dah and I know you think I am insane.* I knelt.

I flung my arms out wide. I didn't know the words. I've always hated Broadway musicals except for West Side Story. I walked sideways on my knees to the next boy, Michael. Little Michael with very thick glasses and a blue baseball cap that was more like a construction hat, hard plastic. Michael's nose was really pointed and he spoke softly like a child. Yes, or no. Not much else. He was like a really sweet little girl with a big belly. Probably in his early thirties. His family visited once in a while. *The wind it comes down to the plains. And the plains are less fun than our games. Soooooooooooo what oh Mr. Fernald. You're lookin' fine Mr. Fer-nald* …. They all just sat there. James, big James in the first chair looked a little scared, but then he began laughing softly, saying little words once in a while…plain, plain.

I had grown up with these songs, every fucking Sunday of my life. Bali hi over here. Here I am your special lover. Come away to my chair. I put my sneaker on the arm of James's chair. He was smiling. A song you may sing for the rest of your life. You may get a swing and you may get a bike. I had both my feet on his armrests. I stepped to Peter's chair. He was clapping viciously. I patted their heads, came in close to their eyes. Kissed a few cheeks. It felt like nobody had ever paid so much attention to them, and for me…I had never been allowed to bellow, sing my heart out—to totally take control of a room of seated men.

Bali hi, I curtsied to them, well actually about three at a time and there were twelve men. I broke down at the end. I collapsed. Prostrated myself on the floor in front of them and looked up. They were all just staring. Staring and drooling. It was simply about me. Which is one definition of insanity. I started clapping, clapping. Leroy got up and took off his clothes.

He was this huge black baby. About six feet tall—no, more. I only remember him in big white undies though once the program got going we put him in green clothes, grey ones that mostly didn't fit and he stood there—one hand, clutching holding the extra cloth that drooped at the crotch, creating sort of a Middle Eastern look. They all looked like this. Wandering around the ward like members of an ancient fraternity, Jesus's friends strolling through a long afternoon in Jerusalem…somewhere in the desert. A little town where men could jabber forever, relaxed, cool.

Fernald *was* the place where you found out if your head was on tight enough. How would you know? Well for one thing you wouldn't fuck Leroy. He had two small scars on his chest where there used to be nipples. Originally Leroy had decent-sized floppy breasts. Which supposedly made him a treat in the last regime. Which was that apocryphal host of Cambridge ministers who ran little churches on the side streets of Central Square, down by Western Ave, where you weren't supposed to go if you were white—which was a pity because there were plenty of big cheap apartments down there, and sometimes if an old lady was black and I picked her up in my cab after she shopped at Purity Supreme in Central Square she'd say, I'm just going down Western Avenue dear. She'd add with a sad smile. Before I drop. And I would drive slow through all those special streets, with tons of kids, and hair stores and jazz clubs and crane my white neck all I liked. It was the unwealthy side of the river.

The ministers were reputed to have had a penchant for Leroy, because he had tits and a dick. A twofer. It became a silent kind of pornography, the endless imputations of what "they" did. To this kid, seven feet tall. Leroy gets bigger as I speak. He was totally cute. His entire vocabulary was bent around an ascending dah. Babies have one word, dah or something like it, and to all number of feelings and phenomena they go dah. Leroy said his own name a lot. Enthusiastically. Leeroy. Two tones, ascending, descending. Like an orchestra leader he cracked a big smile when he was done. Sometimes smashed his powerful fist on a serving table. Bong! Le-roy! In his infancy he had just broken through to language and everything else moved on and language and his brain stayed right there. He was seventeen. With the vocal chords of an adult male. The strength of a high school football player. Jet black in his bright white underpants. He was something to do at work.

# 5.

Being a kid was also a job. You lived in a house with your brother and sister. They bring in their friends and it becomes a new association. Early on my brother's friends were tall and they imagined themselves Nazis. They had a passion for World War II and saluted each other zig heil. My sister called one of his friends Seal Master. It must have sounded like "zig." We were fond of debasing ourselves in my childhood. Not to each other but perhaps to these next of kin, my brother's friends. It wasn't like you would get totally stuck with them. It was entertainment too. We all laughed at this game my sister and Charlie had. He would speak to her in this sleazy diction and she would say yes Seal Master. Charlie Lemon called his own sister Jew-Anne. She was fat and regarded as really bad news. Charlie Lemon had a high giggle, was fat like my brother Terry, and was supposed to be really smart. Then the parents made friends too.

Both my parents had older siblings they were always trying to get away from. Which contributed to the feeling I grew up with that my parents were not adults. That family was a trap. Uncle Ed and Aunt Florence would come over on Saturday nights and my father would groan and we would all wind up sitting around the kitchen table listening to them.

Ed talked about his suits ("Brooks Brothers"), their stereo (some Japanese name), and on and on, an interminable recitation of all the better products which they owned. It was an irritating display of the wealth of people who had no kids. We sat there, evidence of our family's poverty, happily drinking in the names of the goods. Because it was obvious to us that we would have these things, unlike our parents. During the evening Aunt Florence would make small remarks alluding to what a bore Ed was. And for that, my parents thought she was great. Thank God for Florence, my mother would say when they left. Florence loved cats and that was the thing we knew about her. And Ed liked cats too—it was what they shared. They had a marriage of convenience, we heard, and when we went to their house in Brookline across from some famous school we heard the Kennedys had gone to, we would see their separate bedrooms and wonder. It was cool. Rather than having no kids, they were kids. Rich ones. Their beautiful building in Brookline with its polished wooden doors and brass buttons and excellent intercom system set my lifetime standard for what a good apartment was like, though it's clear I've spent my life, unlike theirs, in a slum.

My mother was terrorized by her sister Anne, who seemed like her mother. Anne was seven years older. They were orphans, Polish ones, and my mother had packed this big suitcase I feel like I've seen I've heard about it so much, to go off and be a nun. Anne, who was newly married to this Irishman, Tim Donnellan, convinced my mother to come live with them in Somerville. My mother's amazing. So, first day of high school in the Irish neighborhood in Somerville, they all go to church and the freshmen's names are called off from the altar and rather than saying Pierscienewicz, which would sound like "son of a bitch," she simply said her name was Preston and the story moved on.

The Lemons were different from my family because they were all reputed to be highly intelligent, geniuses. The implication was that we were smart, but that was all. Mrs. Lemon talked so rapidly her hair stuck out straight in an anxious permanent, and she smoked a lot, and nervously ran the ship. Mr. Lemon was the real nut. He went to MIT which was unlike anyone I'd ever known. Supposedly he had a nervous breakdown. Which was sort of the explanation for why the Lemons rented a house in Arlington, and maybe "Big Chuck" was in sales, something risky though he had been trained in school to be an engineer.

I remember our family following their car one summer night and being really excited and scared. We were going to the greatest place in the world, over by Fresh Pond—a place that was dedicated to games, night-games, and it was outside. The place had rifles, BB guns I guess, and also archery. I remember the tattered targets, millions of holes. I remember being big enough to pull a bowstring back and earlier when my father helped me.

We were all out there on a summer night, my parents with their cigarettes and the light being a special color that was not blue or anything at all, just light when it should be dark, a color unearthly, so bright and cool in terms of the extended freedom now for everyone. It seemed that even my parents felt it and there were extra things to do since it wasn't dark. It was like a carnival, the shooting place we went to at Fresh Pond, but more permanent. Of course it's been gone for years. It simply addressed that special urge to hit something with a gun or an arrow while you had a long view and it still wasn't dark. Pulling a trigger was how you said it—even, killed that long cool feeling. Bulls eye! We won, *bang*, and the prizes were made out of joy. Orangey day-glo. Blue animals, soft and fuzzy. A succession of bells. Things vanish and flicker in my memory. The excitement feels eternal, comes back all the time now the older I get. The rewards of my childhood, the feel of it, are stuck in the crevices of everyday. A slice of pizza is a blast when I realize that nothing's wrong. I stand there, grease dripping down my chin, stupid and happy, hanging in the light.

Following the Lemons was wild because they had a car that was powerful, a V-8 engine, a green car. Oh yeah big Chuck likes a car to *go*, growled my brother. It was an appreciation of manhood, also a recognition of a nut, a weirdo. Jesus, Ted, we can't do this, said my mother sucking in her breath. Which was a challenge to Dad, so naturally we followed. The Lemons took pills for their nervousness, they were high-strung people, and we only went out with them this one night and I'll remember it all my life. We didn't know what was going to happen. It was this strange man—and a whole other family—way up there, and despite my mother's complaint, Dad drove on.

# 6.

It seems people go nuts from a number of things: being too smart or someone being gone. My father's mother went crazy because her daughter died. Helen, who would have been an aunt if I had ever met her, had appendicitis and she went into the hospital. Helen was getting operated on and peritonitis set in and she died on the operating table. My grandmother would walk the streets at night crying, Helen, Helen. So they put her away in the State Hospital where she spent the rest of her life. We would go up to see her once a month. She called me Helen, and my brother Teddy, which was my father's name.

Once my grandmother gave me a present. It was all wrapped up in aluminum foil, I had never seen a present wrapped like that, though it made perfect sense. It was a red plastic purse with a zipper, and plunging forward I opened it and found a dollar. It was the most unexpected piece of money I had ever received. I never owned a dollar before and the shock of getting it from someone else who I didn't think of as having money was tremendous. I was in the backseat of the car when I opened the purse. I felt very alone. The dollar had magic. I had it for a while. It seemed like no matter what I did I still hadn't spent it. Was that the truth? Maybe I left the dollar in the purse and long after it was gone I would look suspiciously inside to see if the purse had grown another.

My grandmother and my father were both surrounded by a magic feeling. For a long time I wanted to play a musical instrument and one day when I came home from school I found a Hohner harmonica sitting on the kitchen table. It was like a discovery, more than a present. It came in a little cardboard box, a complicated box like a cake with layers and different sorts of cardboard for different purposes, but ultimately the box protected, it made a home for the harmonica. It was a German thing. Which I loved.

I had a teacher who led a puppet-making class at Fidelity House where I hung out after school. She had very straight medium length light brown hair and she wore glasses and I think she had some kind of mole on her face. She wore pearls. She told me about her childhood and made drawings of the kind of backpack she used when she was a child and they all slid on their butts on these backpacks in the snow after school. She made me love an entire country, Miss Ursula, and my harmonica was from Germany too. It was just like the past, in a good way, and the harmonica glowed with secrecy. I grabbed it off the table, knowing it was mine. It was covered in strange old drawings, group portraits on the box. Blue and red, it said Marine Band. You could write for an instruction manual and I did. A booklet came which showed by a series of arrows going two different ways meaning, blow, draw, how to play Negro spirituals. Then my father told me that his mother, Nellie had played the harmonica. I had to get in and see where she lived.

David suggested that I go to Westborough—now, as an adult, and get the records and find out what happened. Did they stick her brain with a needle? Like Frances Farmer. Cause that's the look in the photographs. Old lady in a scarf, her head aimed toward the camera, the mouth open and her tongue looks stupid sitting there. She's been nobody for years. There's hundreds of pictures of that. Weirder still is me, upstage, in the flowing grass of the hospital grounds—a growling child face, imitating Nellie.

# 7.

I was sitting in my aunt's kitchen in Somerville—this is when the whole world had a linoleum floor—and Eddie Martin, this skinny bald guy leaned down to me, pursed his lips and said: "How's chances?" Eddie was my sister's godfather. He wanted a kiss, but I didn't get it.

It happened all the time. Adults were always putting word combinations together, saying something quickly and enjoying it, having a big chuckle for themselves, when it was apparent I didn't have a clue. What did he mean? I sounded it out. "How's." I understood that. Then the "chanciss," almost "Francis"—then I got it! How's Janice? He meant Janice Oaks, my friend Christine's mom.

So I took a stab at it. It was like travelling in a foreign country, growing up in my family. The kitchen was very bright and all the adult faces surrounding me were red and merry. I looked at Eddie with a jolt of understanding. You mean Christine's mom? The adults were keyed in now. Whaat, went Eddie. I was a funny and stupid girl—Jesus sliding on a banana peel in the temple. *Janice Oaks*, she lives on my street. You know her? Eileen, my mother goes, rescuing me, putting the icing on my idiocy. What are you talking about, she sighed. And smiled kissing me on the cheek. The adults turned away. I burned.

Forty years later I'm reading poems in a large café in Santa Fe. Really a bakery, and New Mexico has the best sky in the world. The audience looked like a stern bunch of dykes and new age people. I was having an anxiety attack—pebbly sweat all over my face. It might've been the lighting. But afterwards, in the smash of people coming up and saying things, there was this woman in purple. My mother's age, but clearly from another class, with her bangs and beads and general look of middle-class woman gone Southwestern—a tad academic too. Hello, Eileen. I bet you don't remember me but I'm Janice Oaks. I haven't seen you since you were this high, she went, and smiled, embarrassed by it.

Are my moments of—practically martyrdom also prophetic? I consider myself lucky. I couldn't have known when I was a kid, standing in the strange medina of my family, that Janice Oaks, whose name had become a badge of humiliation, would one day turn up in my real life and say hello.

Janice was long remarried but the husband she had in the fifties was named Dave. He was tall, had dark hair and always wore a cap, that flat-top kind. Dave's cap was beige or maybe pale yellow. Like a soldier's day off. He wore a white teeshirt as did all dads and he had a stiff look around his jaw which was cute, and also cruel. Dave was an engineer. He never spoke. My friend Christine was his kid and she was sick so they moved someplace cool, Cocoa Beach. Dave's engineering was later explained as "rockets" and when my own interests moved to outer space, I couldn't get over that we once had a player living on my street.

Christine had an older sister named Barbara. There was a hurricane at the end of our street when I was five, and I looked out the window at the trees blowing round—the name of the weather was Hurricane Carol, I heard it on teevee. Down the street was Barbara Oaks, so tall in her light blue rubber raincoat standing out in the middle of it. Barbara's out, I cried to my mother, wanting to be in the Wizard of Oz. Well she's big, said my mother. She sure was.

The families I knew were like little boxes. The Oakses were one-two-three houses down. They had a little brother too, so they were girl-girl-boy. People were glad to get a boy in the end. It was like the family paid off. My family got it perfect right away. Terry was planned, and so was I.

One winter night when my father was good, they broke the rhythm. Since my father was a mailman, good meant that even though he was working overtime for the holidays at South Postal, he did not drink, so everyone got their cards and we had Bridgid. My sister was the child of something worse than despair, I guess absence. My dad was pretty gone by then. And my mother followed him, raging, into that abstract place. I remember him handsome and kind, before the growls began. That's what the late stages of alcoholism sounds like. A person growls, they're not human anymore. They just don't want to know.

It's definitely why I was able to work in one shitty institution after another. It didn't matter where I was. The world was a little like home. I was educated in these places too. In my childhood I often got the message that I was a worthless little animal.

But Bridgid was something else. In a family that didn't think much, by the time they got to her they didn't think at all. For a godparent they tossed her Eddie Martin which who like a too-rich dessert. He stuffed her with gifts and sweets and then he died. It was a little worse than that, but as a result Bridgid was even more deprived than the rest of us. Terry was actually better off than me, but that's how men are raised. They're deluded. They get the idea that they are more important, than, say, their sister. Then they go out into the world and discover that other men are more important than them. So of course they go home and slug their wives. I'm not saying that's true of Terry, but you know, men.

Late one afternoon I was climbing over a stone wall that separated one yard from the next. My town's identity was in flux when I was growing up, but there were still plenty of ye olde elements that added texture to our play. Houses were frequently old, though never as old as the graveyards. Everything was loaded with rocks and I was climbing over the boulders, that surrounded a bright green backyard and there was Georgie Wilson, a boy who quacked like a duck, cutting my sister's hair. One of her braids was already on the ground. Bridgid stood there politely, as if some older wiser person was doing what they could to make her beautiful. Both of these kids were wearing glasses. My sister was cute, but she didn't know it. Nobody ever told her. She was always mad as hell.

Georgie Wilson had a cleft palate and he was my sister's friend. As the second child in my family, I hated injustice and had a strong sense of compassion. I really felt these things, and if I wanted to be anything when I grew up, I would be a prince and fight for good. But I was a kid, we stuck together, and the most powerful glue of the gang was being cruel. Georgie was an easy mark. He quacked. There was a day in my neighborhood when all the girls wanted to pull a boy's pants down and it was Georgie's we got. I remember his bare little white ass looking exactly like a girl's. I don't even remember him having a penis, we weren't interested in that.

He wore very thick glasses, had had several operations to fix his condition, and his upper lip was all scarred—it went right into his mouth and there was a hole in the roof of it. That's what cleft palate meant. He was older than Bridgid and I remember his little boy teeshirt with stripes. It was brown striped and I saw how vulnerable his little chest looked underneath it, and he wore a baseball cap and when we pulled his pants down he cried. I knew we were doing something really sick when I saw that. His mother came running out from someplace. As usual, we were stopped.

Georgie submitted to us just like he did to his operations and his mother was a tired-looking woman with a permanent, just like mine. I came over the wall yelling stop. Bridgid shook her head like she just woke up. They were playing barber. I walked my sister home, carrying her pigtail. Then my aunt gave her a permanent. Now we all had one. Bridgie was the only kid on the block that Georgie could top.

# 8.

I used to go to this place called Fidelity House. I was a member, I had a card. My membership card was hard plastic, with rounded edges. Clack, if I dropped it. It was ruby-colored with a matte finish. It had my name on it. With this card I took all the classes I liked: ceramics, Miss Ursula's puppet-making class, clay, and of course drawing. At drawing I was the best. I mean, the best I got. I drew a lot at home. I drew all the time. The year my father died I had apparently graduated. Mrs. Lester, the teacher, who I loved a lot, but actually wasn't a very good artist herself, but loved kids drawing, asked me to be her assistant. I was thrilled. There was no pay. Then he died. We weren't poor, but I felt that the way to be closest to my mother was to get a job, to do anything to support myself, because now that I was half an orphan, I was more like her. I got baby-sitting after school, no more Fidelity House, I could make about five dollars a week and I could save and buy clothes. I remember the day I told Mrs. Lester. I was really afraid. I thought she would be mad, and miss me. She looked at me nervously. Okay Dear if that's what you want to do. I walked down the street crying, walking home. I wondered what being her helper would have been like. I swung my bag. Let the babies help themselves. Art is for kids.

# 9.

The behavior modification program at Fernald was a big hit. The dicks were all tucked in, the boys had stopped peeing on the floor. Pretty much. So we put a ribbon around each one of their necks with a metal ring on it and when they continued to succeed we gave them a token. A small flat brightly colored piece of plastic with a hole on one end. It looked like a tiny hot dog. The guy clicked it onto the ring. Instead of candy they got this. At first it was distracting enough to work. You could see them wondering where the M&Ms went, but the new element was fascinating and confusing. Big James would just pop the token on and go, what else. In a silent, nodding, blinking way.

Else was toy planes. A whistle. Little Napoleon holding his pants up with one hand, twirling around with a red plane in the air going da-da, da-da. We helped him cheat. The vision up at the Shriver Center was a token economy, a system of rewards with which, once we got rid of all the bad behaviors, we could start building new ones—the boys making beds, getting dressed pronto, all shining faces walking towards the imaginary store in the sky, where they would turn their tokens in for the privileges of every man—planes and whistles, maybe even getting a job, ultimately even beginning to understand money. But it didn't work.

For every guy like James who just popped it on, or schizophrenic Walter who was now over by the window, dancing and talking to himself, with a necklace of plastic tokens flapping around his neck, there was someone like Napoleon who could barely get one token on the ring. It was just too damn hard. He would grunt and hit the ring with the flat token, sweating and twitching, again and again, never looking up, crying soundlessly, and sometimes accidentally doing it, but never understanding and doing it again. Then seeing the other boys with their planes, crying, crying till we rigged the sport. I never knew what happened after that. I moved to San Francisco.


Art class was the saddest part of the day. I used to open the closet door and bring the cigar box full of crayons over to the table, and I put the papers down and got everyone who would do anything at all to sit at the tan formica table and begin to draw. Michael in the blue construction helmet liked black. Every day he took his black crayon and began drawing a wiggly line on the left side of the paper and he brought it across. Until the paper was covered. Then he put his crayon back in the box. He closed it. He picked it up and carried it into the closet. Put the box on the second shelf. Shut the door. Flipped the latch shut. Hung his little head down and walked quietly back to the table and folded his hands. His eyes would roll around the room, then down. Michael was so sweet. He wanted to stop everything.

# 10.

There are some things I need to tell you about the little girl, her education. It's a parable, and eventually the parable rots.

Because she learned to read in the maternal way, that is, because her mother was a good reader and performed her starring role in the early evening on the corner of her kid's bed, the girl was a good reader too. She learned to read from the flipped pages and the long meditations on the pictures in the book and the squiggle of a number on the corner of each page, and then words—the printed rows of talk, the chattering march of letters, pushing right up to the edge of the page, but not falling off because the mother talked on, and then the girl knew the story too.

Part of the story was in the picture that faced the page and the girl knew how the picture sounded and what it looked like when she saw it on the next page, and the mother turned it. She and her brother would say the words along with the mother and then the mother started to say I'm not going to do this anymore. You already know this story.
And they would cry, please please.
You're too smart for me, you kids, said the mother.
Teach us to read, they cried.

I already did! she said
Really, they laughed, and started saying the story again.

When they got to school it was so tired and slow, learning each letter little and big, one by one instead of the word, the picture's name. Kids would write it slowly on the board and in their books and on their paper slowly, but there it all was, already up there, along the edges of the blackboards—letters and words. The best part of school was reading aloud. She loved it.

In the big hollow school room in the morning, after watching her breath like a cartoon all the way to school, pinched glueberries with her mittens and they were sticky and stained, and morning was almost over, the cold was gone, and she was entirely warm and ready for lunch, they did it.

One by one a kid stood up when his name was called on flash cards. They would stand there, boys in their corduroy pants and girls in navy blue "jumpers," the nuns called the uniform.

She was excited waiting for her name to be called. It took her breath away. Really slow she'd stand up. You had to know your place in the reading. She did. The room was quiet now. "The girl ran. Faster and faster. Come home, Jane. Come home, Jane, the mother called."

"Kevin Coughlin."

The girl was so sick of standing up and reading perfect and the nun going, "Kevin Coughlin." He got up and she sat down. He was dumb. Anyone who was in her brother's class and now in hers was dumb. Kept back. Usually they peed on their clothes, or got mad in school, acted crazy and laughed a lot. They were in trouble. They were big and ashamed.

Kevin Coughlin took all day.
It's Jane, Kevin, *Jane*.
Not Jean.

*Faster*, just like it was before.

Same word, Kevin. Don't be afraid.

Then one day the girl decided to stay up longer, so she had to trip and stumble like he did and the nun would go, that's a big word, Eileen. Sound it out. Like me. Look at my mouth, Eileen. Some-thing.

She got to the word, already reading a little slower than usual, creeping up so it wouldn't be like all of a sudden she couldn't read. Maybe she was tired or sick. She was dying. "Some—" The girl shook her head a little bit and left her mouth open like dumb kids did. She loved thinking of everyone who was looking at her this long.

"Some—" She started it again. "What is wrong with you, why are you pretending to not know that word? Don't you know you are being ungrateful for your God-given gifts and flaunting them, being a clown, not a lady. You should be ashamed of yourself. Sit down.

"Kathleen Reedy, pick up after 'something.' "

When the girl got to sixth grade, the nun passed out these science brochures from the public high school and explained that the students were probably too young for these but maybe some of them would find it interesting. The girl found it very interesting because she intended to be a scientist, but probably she was too young and would continue on with her own microscope for a year and maybe do something like this next year. When next year came she was scared that they wouldn't pass them out because she was ready now and saw them on the nun's desk and was so excited.

The brochures sat there for days. One day before the bell rang they were in quiet time to do homework and the girl raised her hand. Yes, the nun said. Are those things on your desk about the science courses...at the public school? She nodded. My mother would like to see one of those. She said I should get one. You don't have to lie about it, the nun said. I don't think your mother wants one. Just walk right up here if you want one. Does anyone else want one. She looked around. I don't know what this foolishness is about!

I'm not lying. Science is my secret, the girl thought.

The Delays lived next door. Eight red-heads. With dogs. They had such a life. Their family was even connected to the fire department. You'd hear the sirens and the Delays all ran out, jumping into cars. My mother's looking down the street shaking her head.

They had a big fat mother, Grace, and she called my mother Mylesie. It was cute—this fat woman out hanging clothes calling my mother that. Once the Delays tied a fishing net to a long bamboo pole and we all went down to Spy Pond to go turtle fishing. That's right. It was so unbelievable. I was barely able to stay in my skin, it was so Huck.

Where can I get one, I asked. I think they said, it's a *net*, you stupid asshole. That's how they talked. My mother worked at Playtime. It's still there in Arlington Center. She was a secretary at a toy store which was pretty cool, but it made me embarrassed going there. You'd just walk in, wanting. It made me feel poor. Deprived. She always threw that word at us when we wanted something. Oh poor you, she said. You're deprived. It was hard to know what we were.

Anyhow, I discovered that Playtime had such a net, but they were all out. Bob said he'd order one. Did he, I asked my mom. How long will that take. Hold your horses, she said. I looked outside. It was spring. It wouldn't be spring long. I woke up each morning looking outside. Looks like another good turtle day. I was gnashing my teeth. I had the dough. I was very good at saving. I called my mother a couple of times at work. It seemed my mother and Bob worked very close. Bob says no, she happily replied. He was a younger guy, I knew he was special. He was like her son. I think he was some relative of Maurie, her boss.

Who was a Jew. Jews were special in that when someone died they came to your house and sat down. My father was dead, just that year, and Maurie had come. We liked him a lot for doing that. Bob was a Jew too. We had this idea that they were related, but maybe not. They were just both Jews. Anyhow at dinner I said, Mom. When is he going to have my net? She lifted her head and glared.

I got on my bike and pedaled one day after school. On my own I went over the bridge at Spy Pond. I went to Zayres.

It was a question of being able to get to where they would have it. I realized it was something I could do. I brought it home. I was sitting on the couch stroking its dark green strings. *Mine.* Where did you get that? My mother said when she walked in. Zayres. She went into the kitchen with dinner on her mind. What am I going to say to Bob, she asked, banging pans. She stuck her head through the doorway and grimaced. I made a problem for her.

She walked up the back door steps one day. She shook her fist at me when she entered the kitchen. It was a theatrical gesture, it didn't mean violence. My mother was a cartoony women. Bob put your net on my desk this morning. I bet Eileen will be thrilled to see this, he called to my mother. I had to tell him you already had it. He was heartbroken. My stomach turned. Eileen he's a *kid*.

Next day, I got a bamboo pole and I stepped outside to go turtle fishing. It was already summer. Warm and damp. Dennis, get that net, said Dickie, leader of the Delays. Our parakeet escaped, yelled Dennis, grabbing my net. He smashed it again and again on the overhanging leaves. Philodendron bushes, those fat ordinary green leaves. My net was torn to shit. I couldn't tell my mother. She would just go: See.

# 11.

In North Building they used those pale green, yellow, light almost grey-blue bowls—plastic ones that the government buys and distributes everywhere in America so that everyone is aware of institutional eating. The clank of it. The metal soupspoon clucks at the bowl. The people who never go outside eat the only thing that keeps them alive and sometimes they just starve for days. Not eating was not considered a negative behavior, and residents were often either out and out pigs or skinny and starving—*sticks*. Angry waving sticks by the window.

Huge vats of watery oatmeal would be rolled in every day at 12:15. Usually my own stomach would be growling and I'd hear the bluster and smell the stink in the halls. It was food. Watery oatmeal. It reminded me of a sweater. A xerox of a sweater you're handed when you need to get warm. It wasn't even tweedy this oatmeal. It was blue grey brown. It was beige, it was grey. It picked up the plastic lights from the side of the bowl. It shimmered like the big metal tubs it came in. Where do they keep the Kennedy girl, I wondered each morning. Does she eat this shit. It didn't come with milk. Where's the milk, George? I asked on the first day.

The milk's in it, George's eyes twinkled. George Barlow. A wonderful man. We had long conversations in the clothing room. We'd be figuring out the boys' outfits early in the day. Grab some pants, a pair of socks. George had this twinkle in his eye and a slightly moist look around his lips. He was incredibly old. 36. He had been at Fernald all his life. He said they decided he was a little stupid when he started school and they sent him here and nobody ever minded and nobody ever found out. Your family, I inquired. One more mouth to feed. George's eyes twinkled as he unknotted socks. He gestured at himself innocently. *I* didn't know any better. I just figured I was stupid too.

After the big shakeup in the sixties, he said, they noticed that I knew what was going on. If anyone asked me anything I'd tell them. Usually they didn't ask. They assumed I was dumb. One of the attendants a few years ago began to teach me to read. It's not so hard. I didn't know *that* was what they were doing. The letters. His eyes twinkled like he meant the letters were doing something. Oh yeah, I said. That.

I'll probably get out of here, he said, looking around. He smokes a pipe, George. And he eats the food. Where's the milk, George? The milk's in it, he told me. Mixed in. It's easier. They don't mind, he assures. I saw a big fat man in overalls pouring it down. He sat in a huge high chair. With the bowl to his lips, looking. Eyeing his friends.

No sugar, I asked George. It's in the coffee, he gleamed. Lifting a see-through plastic cup of coffee and pouring some onto Peter's cereal. Thanks George, Peter slurred. Some mornings I wanted their oatmeal but I had already been there too long. I mean you could try the oatmeal in your first week when you didn't know anything yet, you could get away with tasting it then, being dumb.

I wanted it. I only seriously considered having it when another attendant was in the room because if I was alone with them and I had a bowl of it I would be one of them. If I had it when George was there it would be like being one of them because he was one of them even though he could talk about it. Once in a while I would have half a cup of their coffee in one of the plastic cups. "See-through" but really you couldn't because they were so old.

They had been washed by big machines, again and again, tall plastic cups that had lived their lives in institutions so now instead of being see-through they were "scratch." That was their color. With ridges for a safety grip. The coffee was beige, sand-colored, grey. It was blue-grey coffee, tan. Flavored with milk, watered down, not much, not real milk. Probably government surplus powdered milk, probably that. So it was grey, like endless land. I drank a half a cup of the stuff. They looked at me, disgusted, whoever I was working with, but they'd done it too, we'd all done it one morning or another, drank their coffee as if it were ours.

Is there a recipe book for everyone? In America, when it comes down to that: here's something for everyone, a book or a cup of coffee, a bowl of oatmeal, that not you or I or anyone we know would ever want to eat, but food that anyone would eat when they had finally been determined to be in that position that they would eat anyone's food. I don't mean eating from the dumpster. I mean the mechanical lunches you got in school. Those vegetables no one wanted because you could see they had been prepared for anyone. Extra food. To think you might wind up eating it one day, looking around, the day you forgot who you were.

# 12.

I think of her when I look at this screen. I say, "Grandma." I was home at Christmas. My mother goes, funny you should mention Nellie, and she hands me this little stack of photo books with plastic bindings, and there she sits in all her crazy goodness. Her head is lowered, back bent, and she's squinting into the sun of the camera, maybe 1956.

The infant in the picture is Bridgie, and Nellie smiles at her. Babies always brought her back, sings my mother. Her hands wouldn't open for years. My mother shakes her head. Now, there's Helen. She was big, I guess she's about twenty-five here...see, said my mother, you're like her. Big features. She looks at my face.

The Myleses weren't pretty women. But look at that chest. I guess Nellie. . . *tsk*, hard to tell. Helen stands with two men. They're having lunch, says my mother. Near South Station. She lifts her glasses. In the forties, I would guess.

The pictures are here so your brother can show his sons. They should know their family history, she says, patting the books. The photos are sitting under a lamp in the den, a room I grew up in.

I grabbed the pictures and brought them home. My father and his brother Vincent are in the backyard, digging. I remember the day. I sat in the kitchen listening to them. They're holding shovels and they're digging a hole. These are not guys who liked to work. It was that fake suburban effort. The picture's so eerie. Both of them would be dead in two years.

That's nice my mother said, and she took the picture.

# 13.

I used to spend hours staring at Peter Pan. A drawing of him. In a little book that I knew the pictures. That lock of boyish hair falling down the front of his face in a way I think of as British.

Almost twenty years ago I became friends with David. He was the smartest man I ever knew. We met in the living room of some friends in New York who were having a collating party. It's how poets put books together. You watch literature happen. Everyone takes speed and puts hundreds of pages on top of each other. David and I kept running out for more beer and got to know each other that way. He had the biggest face I'd ever seen. Long like Easter Island. He spoke in many languages and he could speak all day. We were buddies.

I thought it was like a male friendship, which I loved. I imagined that he was a centaur, or even a wise old crone, and I was the sweet young warrior. Definitely, David educated me. I would call him at work. I'd ask him a question, and he would reply. That would be Propertius, I believe. Here, let me send you something.

Finally, he introduced me to a friend of his who actually inspired the story of Peter Pan. This was living fantasy. The man's brother was "John," the kid in the glasses and top hat. I never heard a thing about Wendy, she was probably imaginary. But he was the baby, the guy I knew.

Tall, erudite and drunken, and like David, he knew all about words. He said that rivers are the oldest names in a place and it's true, look at a map. James Barrie was a friend of their parents. A world of nannies and theater. Barrie was queer of course. All the best-loved children's books are written by us, queers of some sort. Look at Lewis Carroll, total pervert. I think the whole reading thing is pretty suspect. The parent sits on the edge of the bed and reads this in-between book that scares everyone, making the child very valuable to the parent, precious, and the kid dependent on the adult, who has meanwhile read them this tale. It's the first erotic literature.

One summer when I was eighteen, I was standing down in the browning yellow of Filene's basement reading the paper. I was looking for opportunities to get out of Boston for the summer. It seemed I could work at a summer camp. I'd make no money, but I wouldn't be here. It seemed like a sin, a crime to work in the city in the summer in the bowels of a department store.

My mother and sister dropped me off at an overnight camp in New Hampshire. Camp Bradley. It's where I met Lucy Bean. Though I was only 18, I was already an adult condemned to re-enact the childhood I had never had. I wanted to go to overnight camp. I wanted to be dropped off by my parents with my bags. As it turned out, I was the youngest counselor assigned to the oldest cabin. I was 18, they were 14. I often feel that this experience turned me into a homosexual.

I would stand in Filene's basement considering the spectacle of my first year of college, school. It bore no resemblance to the future I had imagined. My present education illustrated how faulty my understanding of life was. I saw it as a series of projected images I would magically begin to inhabit. The images were based on the past—college, some bunch of bright young people in sweaters dashing up the steps to their astronomy class, something I saw on teevee—Ozzie &

Harriet college, because no one I knew had ever gone. So when I began college, the future was dashed to bits by the present.

Now, it meant suburban buses connecting to the T and then down into the red line and the orange line and the green line to a bunch of reclaimed buildings in Park Square—Salada Tea, the Old Boston Gas Co.

We would sit in Patsio's and drink our bleary morning coffee and see the first street people we had ever laid eyes on. An old woman pulled up her skirt for us and showed us her bald old pussy. We were going to school. There was an Irish bar around the corner where we'd go after jazz class and smell stale beer and a trio would play there on Friday afternoons, a really old man and a really old woman and some third thing, I can't remember, but I know it was a trio. They were so drunk the music was incredibly bad, and the only point to them was that they were old, so old that it was hilarious that they would try to pull off this kind of late afternoon soft-shoe entertainment, and one afternoon they weren't there because one of them had died, and that was that. This could not be college, it was something else. Actually it was an introduction to bohemia, the seedy, the demi-monde. So things were really as prophetic as they should be.

I remember the smell of Sullivan's. Sweet decay. There was a guy not much older than me who usually wore a suit jacket and white shirt and was enamored by City Hall politics and he always seemed to be in some kind of energized fog and it was later explained to me, because sometimes I'd see him take his jacket off, that he was an alcoholic, his drinking was a problem. How could somebody's drinking be a problem, in that old person's way already? I thought it was because of the way he dressed and the things he cared about. There was no campus. It was not school. I would sit in class and look for men that mattered, someone who belonged there as little as I did. I had chosen the school for its name. University of Massachusetts sounded all right. It wasn't, but I was living a life that I wrote, all these disappointing and confusing things would be perceived in a book, one that was read, and then it would be okay, the world I was in. I imagined a book that forgave.

Because I could see that I was lost. Already, I had given up on college. I would continue to go to my classes and get a degree, but its meaning was open, it was simply happening, that's all. I know the present occasionally engulfs you and you stand there saying, hey this will be the future, but you're wrong again, it's the present. It was like that with the Doors at Crosstown Bus. The lights blinking on the walls, the erotic man singing. A girl slightly skipping and swaying in a skirt with her eyes half-closed in a way I could only faintly understand was sexy to me, but everything was carried in a wash of the already gratified request to "Let me sleep all night in your soul kit-chen," the meaning only barely breaking through. I was trying to contain her as Snoopy, the dancing girl with the man's voice reeling on, which was me. I sat in class and thought maybe him, maybe him. I was looking for a man to take me out, not literally, but who I could kind of ride with in a parallel universe like the dancing girl and the man's voice which I saw in my head again and again. It was kind of like my family who were never really there, where we were, but kind of about something else, like Martians. I wanted to go home, where I had never been.

This man, Peter Whitman, was sitting there in class, German class, and he was sort of blondish brown-haired, tan complexion, slightly older I suspected, maybe a vet. One day I was sitting in the park. Our school was near Boston Common, the Gardens. If I sat there on a green bench reading a book, I was somewhere between lunch on a part time job and being on a college campus. Sometimes I would watch the swan boats, be bothered by men, not much, and sometimes I would watch crazy people and feel sick. I was drawn to normality. The American institution. Peter Whitman walked by. Big boots, that suggested he had been in the military. They all were like that, veterans, they all had one thing they held onto—the jacket, perhaps. My father was like that too. I remember a gun in the front closet, a helmet. My mother would threaten us with his belt. Hi, I smiled. He sat right down.

I can remember what I had on, an odd stretchy shirt with a collar and long sleeves but really tight and I rolled the sleeves up. It was dark blue but it faded and it was covered with swinging designs, like those boomerangs on formica table tops. They reminded me of the future, of atomic energy. Hi, he said. His face was tan and that's what I was doing. Tanning. At least you didn't have to look like the people in your school. Peter Whitman was out here too. Our orbits collided. I can't remember a word we said, but he was an adult. I figured something would happen after that, a date, but it didn't. Nothing happened. He was just an image.

All the girls in my cabin, Birch Lodge, had been to Europe. It felt weird. They could swim, they could ski, they had been to France and rode horses. The person most often miscast in my movie is me. The other counselor in my cabin was Dale. She was from New Canaan. You know I don't want to tell this much of a story. Dale, the tennis counselor. Short, stocky, Italian, a peasant type, with kind of something wrong with one of her eyes. I hated her. Maybe her pupil was gone in one eye. It was kind of all smeary blue. She was so *good-natured*.

I want to talk about that word for a moment. Swinging by trees in the car one day when I was barely an idea, very young. It was my mother and another woman—not familiar, then my brother...I was looking at the green of the trees whisking by like when you lie down in the back seat. I was thinking about the green. Terry's a fat pig, I yelled out. We had company so I was testing what I could do in this altered setting. Maybe he would punch me or something. Terry smiled serenely which was sickening. He was showing off. He's so *good-natured*, groaned the woman in the front. I remember my little body filling with rage. Good-natured had to do with trees, which was not like Terry at all. He was like stones. Food. Glue. Meanness. I was "imaginative." She has such imagination, some other lady said to my mother and I thought it was the time to point this out. "You should see some of the things I think up," I yelled out now. I was filled with the excitement of myself, my words, my ideas. I was nothing but breath and pride. Eileen, shush, said my mother. Terry smiled. Pretty soon we stopped, went someplace. Maybe Westborough, but I felt I was born that day, it's so vivid and new, the words and the feelings and pictures. The green, speeding and natural.

In the morning Dale would come and touch my tits. She would come over and do this and I would pretend I was asleep and I would think of various people who it would be more interesting if they touched me in this swirling way, and I would fall back to sleep in a moist heat of sexual imagination. Always in these morning episodes I am a boy. When I lie there being touched by Dale or anyone else. It's like I've looked at pictures of boys, Peter Pan, some young prince in a mustard-colored jerkin in a framed picture on a wall at the Martins' house. I've dreamed about these boys' erotic potential in the hands of bossy girls for so long I go right into a fugue state and join their ranks at the touch of a girl's hand. Though sometimes I am her. The girls in Little Women undressed Laurie on a regular basis and forced him to wear certain dandified outfits which were cuter, but conflicted with his stern sense of masculinity which was at war with his prettiness. This was a secret passageway I found in Louisa May Alcott's novel, and I elaborated on it endlessly for my brother, who would frantically whip through the pages of the old red book and look for my strip scenes to no avail. My brother and I aroused each other verbally for years. In my family we talk a hot fuck. My brother's stories were true life adventures participated in by girls we both knew and these stories could never be authenticated. Mine were simply literary since I was such a baby I felt that no one would include me in the truth. I was glad to be a baby if I could be a boy undressed by many humiliating girls. After I began settling into life in Birch Lodge, Lucy arrived. I don't remember her parents at that point but I can stick them in now. A tall dark haired man in white shorts, and a sandy haired woman, nothing spectacular. Nice, nervous-looking. In their thirties, I guess, right? Lucy was their kid.

I want one, I thought. She was adorable. A perfect girl boy. It was like in that moment I transferred my account from me to the world. I began to look out.

All I can remember about Lucy is a report I wrote. It was such a failed summer. I got a job as an arts & crafts counselor but I didn't know how to do anything. We had this big loft with a kiln, and tons of paints and high eaves. It was paradise. I wanted to get right down to work, draw and paint. Unfortunately, I was stuck with them. I remember my partner, Joanie McLean, who seemed like a teacher or a librarian. Not an artist like me. Eileen, go look at their work, she'd shove, and I'd shuffle around the loft, making cracks, being their cool older sister. Though Joanie was furious, I'd managed to convince her that she could do half the class, I'd do the other, and the assignment invariably arrived in her half, work time in mine. I'd always work too, and we'd talk a lot. Me and the girls. But mainly I was not into being there at all, it made me so sad that I was not an artist, had not gone away to school, or overnight camp. I'd put on my bathing suit and pout. Or rather, tan. As usual I was on a diet. I was best at being still. I was an endless teenager, striking a pose, being brilliant at that, at least. I brought a lot of books to camp. I was reading the trilogy. (Tolkien.) Having applied sufficient baby oil, I would lie down in my bikini on a lounge chair in the big porch around the main hall. I would listlessly read in the afternoon, occasionally one of the counselors going by giving me shit—taking a little time off, Eileen? I would smile and flip them the cover of my book, the trilogy. *Cool.*

Occasionally Lorette Wilson or Mitch would walk by. They were the boss couple. He had a crew cut, wore a white teeshirt and big chinos. Was an art teacher, ceramics, during the school year. It was their camp. Mitch was a handsome man; Lorette was butch, big glasses, jamaicas, thick muscled legs and carried herself as if she'd been in the military and now we were too. I was spotted as a loafer right away. Who could miss it. I thought reading a book was good, I thought getting a tan was, I had never even imagined that such a low paying job carried the burden of an ethos, that I had consented in some way to wear the camp uniform all day, green & white right from the moment of morning flag salute. Birch Lodge here. I hadn't realized we were theirs. I mean I read an ad in the *Boston Globe*, Camp Counselors Wanted. I got an application in the mail, I filled it out and returned it and they congratulated me that I got the job. And now for a stipend of $250 they own me from morning to night. You've got to sneak around, one of the other counselors informed me. I didn't get it. I had an inferior sense of work. An hourly rate, nothing else. I certainly didn't understand conduct, not patriotic conduct. Not Protestant patriotic conduct.

"Blood 'n' guts," spouted Lorette, after a whiskey or two at the cookout. That's what this country was built on. "I hate blood and guts," I spit back, having had a few beers myself. "Well you better learn to love it if you're going to get anything done in this life. Nothing gets done without a lot of sweat and effort," she said nearly seething at me, and I felt this had to do with lying around in a bikini, and she never spoke to me again after that. Certainly never said my name. Occasionally a crisp hello which merely served to grease her stride as she marched around surveying her lands in the course of the day. In her gaze all of us were connected. There were a few extras—the cooks: the Derbys, who had sad beagle eyes, and their boy, Tony, who played alone and looked sort of dumb. They had a little house of their own. As did Margie and Carl, our couple. They were recent graduates of Colorado State, having both majored in speech pathology, and Carl was going on to get a advanced degree. Dr. Carl, Margie would joke. He spoke only in the most softest tones about the meaning of his work and his dedication to healing speech defects. He himself had one, had stuttered as a child. Margie had long black hair and dragged Carl's name out affectionately like she were some trashy wife, Cah-rel she would cry (as if she enjoyed being debased by their love), and we, the interested teenagers and young college students were all in on their secret. They fucked. I suppose plenty of us did too and it was no secret at all, but their youth and their beauty and their common goal...! One night drunk Margie confessed that she and Carl were going to start a "center" together. We were in awe, all our faces glowed around the campfire, and Margie's revelation of their plan only added a religious fervor to their fucking—here we were at an extremely straight all-girls camp and they were inside of their cabin having all that, now and in the future. We were immersed in their sex when she said Car-ul.

So what would I do with Lucy Bean? At the end of the summer, or whenever the kids left, we had to write up a report. I mean, it wasn't a big deal. Certainly not to normal people. You don't picture people down at the police station laboring over depositions. Insurance companies don't sweat bullets over accident descriptions. I don't know. Maybe they do. My grandmother died four decades ago and for almost two years now I've been engaged in extracting from the medical records department of Westborough State Hospital a copy of her story. A story? Could it be that?

*Nellie Riordan Myles*
Died 1957, Westborough State Hospital, born in County Cork. So reads: "She lay over the body of her sleeping son, John (Eileen's god-father), and it was approximately 9:30 AM when any decent eldest Irish son would be sitting at his desk, winking at his secretary, feet comfy in his shiny Florsheims, imagining how he would overhaul the part of Boston that lay down around him, ten flights below—Scollay Square, a worthless part of town, and he, John Myles, would smash it to bits with its burlesque halls (The Old Howard—Busty Russell, Cupcakes Cassidy, Irma the Body), tattoo parlors and two-bit whores and kids skipping school, reshaping it into a feasible harbor-front setting with tall apartment buildings and restaurants. All because of her. His beloved mother, Nellie, whose photograph was on his desk on Broad Street.

Instead, John stunk like Old Thompson (Rye), hadn't a woman in his life or a pot to pee in and after all the years of taking guff from his father, Nellie just wanted to kill the slimy bastard, her son John, how she rued the day she had popped him out of her own pained guts. She grabbed the front of his three day-old shirt and yanked him up with the butcher knife in her right hand, placing it under his chin...."

*She said, John, get a job!*

I mean, I would gladly settle for a clear description of how they lobotomized, hydrotherapied, electroshocked Nellie. But probably it's just a death certificate and a scrawled doctor's note. "Patient is melancholic. Refuses to speak, eat."

Because I have spent my life within the walls of institutions, because I was unable at five to get beyond the tulips of the place and see where she lived, I continuously shoot my wad, make my own inappropriate nature vividly plain, endlessly expose the full dose of my abnormality when presented with any simple request to fill out a form that has longer than a one line blank. If there is no form, then I will really go to town and that is what I did with Lucy.

I was not asked by Camp Bradley to do a portrait of her. I was not requested to psychoanalyze her. To adore her. To declaim my love, explore the intricacies of my obsession, to quietly explain that I had spent my life dreaming of girls who looked like boys, that I was one, and had finally found my match, my sister, my little brother. You are taking her away. The summer is half over. I am 18. I came here because I weigh one hundred and thirty-three pounds and live in Arlington with my mother brother and my sister and my father is dead and I drink too much. Nothing is ever right in my life. I have no desire. I only want clothes and to be somewhere else. I have been hidden so long, my life is over and yet it has hardly begun. I stood there within the yellowing walls of a department store where I was more at home than in the hulking corridors of the state university that did introduce me to a larger intellectual framework than I had ever imagined existed. Yet I still hoped college would be a place where I would be transformed—by the very walls of its institutional beauty, by its otherness, by its relationship to a purer existence than anything that I had ever known, a world of intelligence and sports cars, of nature and science, of bits and pieces of all the wisdom known to man in handsome leather binding, books and stone and freedom, the Ivy League, other states, western ones, small mid-Atlantic junior colleges, strange art schools in California, anything that, unlike me, had managed to put its roots in a suitcase, a trunk, and got on a train and went away. I was not like that and I had come here to Camp Bradley in my shame and with what tiny hope I still allowed myself, perhaps to find a way to assemble something that would do just as well. Art. To make something like it. A semblance. To rekindle my dream. That I could put on a pair of shoes, have a small job and walk around in a new situation and improve myself a bit, and change.

Fat chance. I had lust. I had excitement and lust over a small child who was perhaps my sister's age, who had a voice like a small harmonica, who had braces and you knew they would come off. Who had small feet. Who rode a horse, but no big deal. Who was a moderately talented artist. Who could see that I was great and admired me for it. Who could see that I was wild. Who saw that in me in the midst of this boring job where I was unable to be a child again, because I had been born wrong, was not encouraged and now was wrong in the world, in the wrong place in it, 18, too late.

No, Lucy loved me. I loved her. Shyly, we walked down the paths through the woods, and I would not have dreamed of touching her, she was more like my religion. But we would be beautiful, I knew that too. I liked her blue sneakers. I loved her little shirts. Even though she was a boy and I was her big sister I could see that she knew I was kind of male too. The sun shone on her hair, like butterscotch and I was in love. This was all wrong. It was so slightly under the surface of every moment in the first half of that summer that I was quietly happy, brighter somehow, I didn't know where the light was coming from. And there were other girls too, it was an all-girls camp, but Lucy was especially mine. She slept in my cabin, she breathed with me. Once I even drew her. I think she took the drawing too. And I would sit with the girls and do clay modeling because I wanted to do her head. I loved her head. I was hiding it. Even from myself. In a tiny bright way I knew. They asked me to write about Lucy Bean. She was leaving camp early. Sure, I said.

"Lucy Bean is so completely charming and intelligent, almost too great a young person to be believed. There is almost nothing wrong with Lucy, and this draws people to her in an uncanny fashion and I would say because of how attractive she is to people and because it seems to come so easy to her to be likable and bask well in the affection of almost everyone who ever lays their eyes on her, I would watch out. I think the one danger in Lucy's personality is that it is really too easy for her to keep pleasing people because that is what they want. I think it might be really hard for Lucy to not do this, to express a little bit of difference between herself and them and I think she should be encouraged to be a little bit ornery."

Her parents were amazed. Every parent of course wants to hear how their kid is the sun around which all kids and lives revolve. I confirmed this for them and even gave them something to watch out for which parents of perfect children need, a little job. I remember the father just standing there holding the paper and his mouth hanging open. "This is amazing. You've really given us something to think about." Now they had their arms around each other. I wonder if they know I'm a lesbian. It was the first time I ever thought that.

Then I went down to my cabin to cry. And I didn't stop eating for two months. I couldn't believe I was in love with a kid. I didn't know I could care so much. She was so perfect. She was the Peter Pan boy. The loss was maybe more gigantic than anything I had ever experienced. Something beautiful was gone and I was exposed. Naked in my feeling for someone else. A pretty little fourteen-year-old girl. At night I would unlock the deep freezer in the kitchen and dig a soup spoon into the peppermint ice cream. I would break open vats of peanut butter. I would get seven candy bars after dinner. There was hole in me I never allowed before. It was a game to see how much I could stuff in. And in this I became sort of a leader. The summer was half over and no one had anyone they loved and it took the edge off those disappointing nights in the knotty pine counselors' room. I remember reading Fail-Safe. Because I always meant to read it. Blaring red cover, black letters. "Raise your dixie cups, the South will rise again." I thought of my fellow counselors as a bunch of college catalogues. There was blonde Kaye from The University of Wisconsin who always wore a green sweatshirt telling us so. She wore glasses and was a writer. There was Julie from King of Prussia, PA who went to Temple and was a Jew. Leslie Rakestraw was from New Mexico, and she had braces because she had been dating a dentist who convinced her she needed them and then he broke up with her.

Her new boyfriend's father was the owner of the Southwestern Brewing Company. He was rich. There was Sue Ellen from Provo, Utah. She had kinky hair, was slightly overweight, had a whole lot of little girl mannerisms and wasn't cute, but was so homely that she was, finally, cute. There was some kind of homo thing going on between us because we got closer and closer, I don't know, we just wanted to tell each other all about ourselves, really obsessive and then she backed off, maybe at about the same time I would have backed off from her and we really never spoke after that. I think she was crazy. I think she withdrew from everybody. Anyway, I learned all about Mormons from her. The relativity of the word gentile was fascinating to me. There's a million stars in the sky. Everyone's other, somewhere. Theresa Jazinowsky, a Pole from Chicago. She was an intellectual. Had a boyfriend named Lenny. They smoked pot. She would do this swaying hippy dance to "I'll be your baby tonight." I think I had a crush on her too. Her father was a working-class man. It was a relief to know that all working class people weren't like me or Dale. Dale never hung out. She popped her head into the room once in a while and embarrassed everyone because we all hated her. The point of all our bonding behavior in the knotty pine counselors' room was that, though we were camp counselors, we were not, in fact, nice people. We were there to be bad. Watching everyone make some transition to sweetness for the brief moment Dale appeared was a kind of falsity I could not bear. She'd only be there for a minute. Had to sleep. She needed to get up early so she could play with my tits and then teach kids tennis. Wonder where she learned.

Something scary was happening to me. I would eat an extra meal and I would jump on the scale. 142. Oh shit. I had never weighed this much. Nonetheless I would bring a huge loaf of Wonder Bread up to the bad room and a cardboard tub of smooth Skippy peanut butter and insist that we all make sandwiches. I brought marshmallow too. It was like the only fucked-up thing you could do. I could get almost anyone involved and was noticing even the swimming counselors soon had little rolls over their bikini bottoms and I knew I was not alone. It was just like I had never experimented with this thing of eating as much as you could. I was just out to smash something as hard as possible. It was like a statue of me inside that I couldn't get out. I decided I would make it huge. Eventually everybody knew something was wrong—I guess we had made it through half the summer and all of us would be going home in a few weeks and I started to get this concerned treatment from everyone that suggested I was maybe going a little bit insane, so I began to socialize, even moderate my eating. Lorette had begun to make comments at dinner that Maw (She had dragged her mother into the camp racket with her, there was a lady we were all encouraged to call "Maw" and she did the book-keeping and the buying for the kitchen. Unlike Lorette, Maw was a tough femme. She wore cardigans over her shoulders, wore a charm bracelet and would have looked normal with a gun in her hand) had decided we should lock the kitchen at night because some counselors were clearly abusing the snacking privileges and green fingerprints were found on the tub of an illicitly opened ten-gallon vat of peppermint ice cream. I had been doing a late night mural for the end of the summer show, The Wizard of Oz, with a particularly big wavering Emerald City and astonished animals striking poses around its gates. Yeah, so (fuck you) it was my fingerprints. The food got locked. It was everything short of being forced to walk the campgrounds with a wooden sign stating "PIG" around my neck.

So I decided to socialize my eating, to diet as had been my plan. I felt like I was lying at the bottom of a well watching the world fall away. If, before, I only had my excess, now I only had my plan. And I knew this plan. It felt tragic. People calmed down around me once they knew I wouldn't incite them to gluttony any more and I guess I started learning how to swim and people were polite to me as I slogged through my six little laps from one dock to another but now I was just kind of holding my breath and I knew something was wrong. You know what it's like to eat seven candy bars, one after another. Well, I no longer had to do that.

One day we went to a Country Fair. It was in Peterborough. We were running a stand with information about Camp Bradley and we had to wear our uniforms which I had finally managed to get into, clipping the little green button closed around my waist. I had been gleefully hopping onto the scales morning after morning, stealthily in the afternoon, late at night. I knew only the morning counted, but now I was living for the sight of those numbers going down, 137, 136 and, Lo! I had arrived at the line of 132, actually skinnier than when I arrived. Who was I now, someone else? Now I would go to an empty stone building at the back of the camp that had a record player and I would make bouillon on the hot plate and Theresa would smoke her Lucky Strikes. And Bob Dylan would croon, *"Shut the lights, pull the shade, you don't have to be afraid. I'll be your baby, tonight."*

We wore these green shorts and white shirts and I don't know if there was anything else. I remember leaning on my counter in a state of…I don't know, if absence felt like bliss, then it could be that. A CIT (counselor-in-training) named Cissy came up and she had a cupcake in one hand and a puppet on her other which she had obviously bought from one of the craft booths. I'm sure it cost 20 bucks. These kids definitely had bigger incomes than most of us. Cissy had braces. H-woh Eileen, said the girl making a voice for a rabbit with a moustache. You don't look very happy. The puppet hands started to grab my nose. I swatted her. Peter Whitman walked by. He was holding hands with a black-haired woman with a ponytail. This was his life. What was he doing here. He had a cigarette in one hand and a woman in the other. He had a dark blue grey shirt on with tiny black things. He had on his big boots. He wore chinos. Did he see me? I turned around. Did he see me. I looked at myself. Green jamaicas. My belly was protruding a little. I wanted a cigarette. No, I will not smoke. I was trying to purify my youth. I wanted to be a perfect sacrament. I was trying to relax. I was trying to not die right away. I was trying to not start clenching my fists. Cissy get me a donut. Get me six. I was trying to stay awake. I was trying to be human. Get me a Coke too. I was trying not to cry. I was trying not to vanish. I was trying to remember who I was. I was trying not to fall down on the ground. Get me a Coke. I want to go. I want to go. Is the summer almost over? In two weeks I shot up to a hundred and fifty-two pounds. The fattest I had ever been in my life. It was like I was nobody. It was like my face was so big. I felt like a big clown. The night of the summer show I agreed to put on a big gorilla costume and I stepped out on the stage and all the kids cheered. I was supposed to frolic and be funny but I just stood there. I wanted to go home. I wanted to hide. I wanted to die. I wanted to not be. I remembered that. A chilly white sound and a picture chilly white from once when I had a fever and bear machines coming toward me whirling and whirling and the insane repetitions of their demands. Do it again Eileen. Do it again. The rhythm of it like a dentist's drill. Not the words, but the syllables. The sound. At the bottom, I was not emptiness, or death. But that. Some horrifying white thing. Again and again. The bear's demand. A whole tribe of them. Or were they gophers. Coming close. Everything white. Their demand.

So Lucy Bean was nothing. She was just me. And she was gone.

# 14.

I got a job in high school at Shore's nursing home. It was a brick building up on Pleasant St. It took me about five minutes to get there from my house, ten minutes from school. It was my first job. Janet Lukas was my co-worker. We had known each other all through grade school. She was a cool girl, having an older brother who was in the cool crowd, so she was second generation cool so she lorded it over everyone. In about sixth grade her and I and her best friend Susie Martel, who was kind of a smart femme, all took ballet lessons together at Fidelity House. Though I had spent my childhood crying for access to music and lessons, special art classes in Cambridge, what my mother deemed would be important for me to take part in was ballet class. Now this is because I was a tomboy and there is nothing more threatening to a tomboy mother than a tomboy daughter. Same with the nuns. The whole world was a plot to turn me into a femme. Many years later when I had my first boyfriend in college, I would confide in him that I was learning to ice skate by watching the man in front of me at the rink, and he screamed in horror that I should not learn to skate from a boy. I would push the sleeves of my sweater up over my elbows and he would laugh and tell me to pull them down. I looked like a man. I was intuitively floating in a sea of male images. I had learned to push the sleeves of my sweaters up from boys and now I was courting the approval of those who would demand I pull them down. It's frightening to think of the excruciating balance in which I've lived my life. Is it masochism? Or simply hiding?

My mother needed me to take the classes so I did. The teacher, Miss Temple, was a ridiculous looking middle aged woman with dyed blonde banana curls. I mean when I think of it, how would any dancer feel who was teaching Catholic children in the suburbs preliminary ballet for 50 cents a week? This is about 1960, so maybe it was cool. I remember her black danskin tank top and tights. I remember a bag that she carried her street clothes in, but somehow she wound up in an outfit that was neither in nor out, which I thought of as dancer, or bohemian. She wore red lipstick. She would encourage us to mime her movements. She broke into a kind of curtsy. One leg would slide forward and she would say something like part a shoo. She would repeat it quickly, pursing her lips, part a shoo, part a shoo. She would go around touching us, adjust our bows. I can't remember if I liked being touched or not. I liked the ballet bar. I liked raising my leg as high as I could and feeling the muscles stretch. I liked anything that made me feel strong and showed me how unbreakable I was. It seemed to be about this strength, ballet, and I liked that a lot. One day Janet and Susie told me they were going to quit. A lot of our friendship in the ballet class had developed through making faces behind Miss Temple's back. She was gross, we agreed. "Red lips," went Janet miming a woman putting on lipstick, as if there were some other way to be. Janet had access to more knowledge through her brother Jackie, so there was definitely something wrong with Miss Temple's lips. I remember the weird feeling of vertigo, knowing that they were quitting and now I would have to quit because I had no way to explain what I liked about the class. The best thing about the class (in my real life—which meant everything outside of my thoughts and feelings) was that it made Janet and Susie like me. The feelings in my legs were too invisible to stand up for. I remember one night watching teevee with my family. It was educational teevee, and there was a man and a woman dancing and the man wore tights and had a big protrusion between his legs which seemed too big to be his penis. It had to be something else. It was part of the costume. It seemed like his sword. I thought it helped him pick the woman up. The woman wore her hair pulled back and had a light short dress on. He would look so cool, holding her lifting her. They wanted me to be her, not him. So, I quit.

The girls we got our nursing home jobs from were Sandy and Karen. Sandy was pale and thin and had brown hair, faintly teased and curled. She just wasn't attractive. She was blah. Karen was blonde, fat, had acne and was the more extroverted of the two. They were both going on to college. Sort of unimportant boring colleges. They would trade the greys and muted reds of our Catholic school uniforms for some empty room in Salem where the state college was. They would be learning to be nurses. So it made sense that they work in a nursing home. Me and Janet needed money, or I did.

So far in my life I had baby-sat, done errands, and sold coat-hangers for money. Hangers three for a penny. My Aunt Anne was a maid at Harvard and she always came home with huge numbers of hangers and I would bundle them and sell them to the Regent Tailors right next to the movie theater. Obviously I would go to the movies with the dough. They were Armenian, the tailors, and I guess they were Jews. Jews were anybody who seemed old and European. Jews were at the dry cleaners, at the tailors, and later at Filene's basement. Anywhere you were selling things there were Jews. And I was always trying to make money and I was always in these slow old places selling things. My family wasn't poor, it was something else. It was that word again—we were "deprived."

The man in the midst of all the cleaning smells and the buttons and the scissors and the zipper hanging around his neck would come over to me and point to certain ones and go, Rusty, no good. They're not all rusty, I'd reply. He would shrug, go, Not so good. Then I would hover, over the counter, getting tenser and tenser. I was waiting for my price. Hovering with my whole body and soul. When it came I could argue with it. Say if he said fifty cents I could say seventy five, and he wouldn't budge. It was a just a way I had of expressing my feelings about the inadequacy of the exchange. I was ten and I had lugged three hundred hangers from Swan Place where I sat in my bedroom after a trip to Aunt Anne's and counted them and banded them with string and carried them over in a bag on the seat of my bike. Today he said, eighty cents, which was pretty good, and I took the money and stepped outside to Medford Street which simply led down to my church and then my school. It was a tiny world, like a toy, and I lived in it and longed to go away. That's what I was selling the hangers for, out of that exact feeling of a need for departure, to be separate, and I wound up sitting in the second row of the balcony with a melting ice cream sandwich in my hand.

Though Janet and I were still underage, fourteen, on the recommendation of Karen and Sandy they gave us our first real jobs. I now had the status, after school, of walking up Pleasant Street with Janet Lukas. Maybe half-way up at the white church we would sit on the stone wall for about ten minutes if we had time and smoke a single cigarette. A Kent. It wasn't like the cigarettes I had with Susie, down by Spy Pond, watching the ducks. We were quiet, we knew we were smart, and at least for me it was romantic and sweet. Without words, we shared our hearts. With Janet it was tough girl bonding. We were cruel. Actually she was cruel, and I knew about cruelty, and of course I knew how to deal it too, with weak kids, but never in school.

So we arrived at this white wood and brick structure, Shore's Nursing Home. Pleasant Street was a wealthy street, with some 18th century houses. That was my brother's department knowing about that, so he could get enraged when he read in the local paper that they were tearing another one down and a group of concerned citizens had gotten together but it was too late. It was the years of watching Arlington change from a New England town to a suburban town. Trees you climbed over rich people's fences were now sweet memories. My whole childhood was dedicated to roving the rich sections of my town, sitting on their white iron benches facing the pond, gazing up at their houses with such great views. Getting permission to fish on their docks. Walking the slow way around the pond, gazing at the island in the center of it, simply trespassing.

It was the Delays who let me know I could do these things; their power came out of their knowledge you could do these things because you were poor. Having a smaller, quieter family, I saw all those things in the world as theirs, the rich people's. The Delays knew we could walk through those doors because the rich people would momentarily feel bad, or encourage us, out of boredom. And then we would push it a little further, because a person wants to expand, and they would say, get lost. What I'm trying to say about the perspective I was given on the world was that there was no way of acting out of a higher sense of purpose, only lower. My family was inactive, fixed, claiming its dignity only in the kind of prohibitions it would practice. We had no power. We were the Myleses. The venetian blinds were down and we were kind of perfect and good. I liked Pleasant Street a lot.

There was a smell you encountered when you entered the side door of Shore's, in the kitchen where we worked. We worked with Mrs. McGowan, the cook. She was a harsh woman who would occasionally smile when she smoked her cigarette. She was probably sexy when she was younger. She carried herself that way. God, did she smell. The food smell was what first hit you when you came in the kitchen door, and it was made in big pans, square metal pans from which she'd ladle the mucousy feast. It was meat and stuff, orange carrots, macaroni casserole, lots of cheese. It was like it was only one dinner, again and again, a pattern of food entering and re-entering a stream of food fabric coming down the line of endless dinner times while we waited for the people to die.

It was determined right away that I would deliver the trays upstairs. The first part of the job was putting faintly plaid trays on the eight rows of shelves that corresponded to floors and beds. Each tray had a napkin, silverware, plastic cup and saucer like the ones I would later see at Fernald. Each tray had a small tin name tag with an old greasy piece of cardboard that said "Mrs. Adams" and so on. Once they were set I would head up to the top floor, the floor with a porch. There was a youngish man who lived in a bathrobe, an old brown wool one, and he had a crew cut and was about my dad's age, in his forties. He had sad blue eyes and he had multiple sclerosis and had food smearing his mouth and moved awkwardly once in a while. He's a sweetie, said the nurse, it's very sad.

I hung out in the hallway near the dumbwaiter and waited for the rattling slam sound down in the kitchen and the crash of the door closing. You'd smell the lousy food arising, ca-chug, ca-chug and when the red light went off you knew it was there. You yanked the door up and there on two shelves was the food. I'd carry the tray into the brown room. There were two or three people in each room. Most days it was only dinner, since we were working after school. In the fall and winter the sun was fading outside and there was a hovering feeling of melancholy. Outside the leaves were falling, it was getting dark, it was getting cold. The man, his name was Bob, was usually smoking, standing, looking out the window of the porch. It was a little chilly on the porch. It had clearly been converted into a room and there was another guy, a really old one, sharing it with Bob and it didn't matter who he was at all, just that the nursing home was mostly women and it was clear that Bob had to share the room with another guy. That's what men did. He was a very successful businessman, it's tragic, said Lois, the tall scary-looking nurse. She was usually who I worked with upstairs, one nurse on each shift.

Lois had a huge beaky nose, salt-and-pepper grey hair combed into something that made her look like a rooster. She was tough, like most nurses were. She smoked a lot, though she wasn't supposed to, and she did her smoking in the hallway, slunk against the wall like a tired waitress. She wore a white synthetic uniform, white shoes and had strong curvy legs. Her eyes were tight and beady and she looked like a huge bird. One of the ladies or whoever would make a sound, a calling sound, and she would look at me, like an animal turns when you both hear something, and she would poke out her cigarette, and strut into the room, leading with a generic baby voice she applied to everyone like angry salve.

I walked in lightly, or as light as I could, and tried to summon up the neutrality of a day in school when I was returning to my seat during a test, not wanting to be seen, but willing to admit I just might be there.

"You're not Karen," said Mrs. Adams. She wore glasses, she was reading a book. "No—" What's your name, she said sternly. Eileen what? Myles. You go to the same school as Karen. You are Catholic. I am not, she said. My name is Mrs. Adams. She extended her hand.

Well, I am very engrossed in my book at the moment, but maybe someday we will talk about what you're reading. Do you like to read books? Yeah. I read a lot. She smiled at me grimly and the conversation had closed. She liked Jane Austen a lot and Henry James. She was writing letters, she kept busy, she was very alone, it seemed. Her stay at Shore's would not interfere with her schedule a whit.

Her roommate, Mrs. Hopkins, was a nut. Hoppy, they called her. She had bushy grey hair going straight up like the Bride of Frankenstein. She was already fairly well into senility. She had a soft vibe, a kind feeling. She had whiskers. The first day I plopped her tray down she asked me point blank, "Are they here?" Who. She kind of looked down and went *whirr*. Back up at me quickly and then she looked away. Back out in the hall, Lois grinned and made the screw loose sign. Wouldn't hurt a flea, she reassured, lighting a smoke. She had her foot parked on the wall to support herself like a girl. The dumb-waiter went clunk and the light went on. Shore's became this strange new punctuation to my day. After school, the momentary longing for freedom. A quick Coke with the kids, and then our walk up the street. We were rarely late since there were two of us coming from the same place.

It's the girls, Mrs. McGowan would purr viciously as we entered the kitchen. Usually old Mrs. Shore was hanging out at that point, shooting the shit with Rita, as she called the cook. Other days Shore didn't emerge until the end. She was close to senile herself, maybe in her mid-sixties, with a strangely unfocused look, soft, but as soon as she opened her mouth and looked at you with those eyes behind thick glasses that were always lidded and squinting, reptilian, you knew that she was totally mean. She never let it out. Everything exhausted her, nothing was worth it. The nursing home was hers. She lived there. She had a son, Fred, and he seemed to help out. He was always coming in with boxes, unloading things, and he was mean too. More awake, with a crew cut. Looked like he had been a marine, dressed like a twink with thick ripple soled shoes. Everything on him was strictly for comfort, but he exuded a soft violent power that was not to be crossed. This evil was never really, well almost never unleashed in my presence, but it was what regulated the day in this place, the repetitive urgency of these miserable people, doing things, the same things, in a place which housed these dying humans and they were making a buck for sure, yet they hated it and you in there with them, their temporary slave.

After I gave out all the meals it was back downstairs and sometimes we had to put up with Mrs. McGowan sitting there in her car-coat, glaring at us, smoking a cigarette. She was waiting for her son to pick her up. As long as she was there we couldn't smoke. Finally she would slam the curtained door behind her, and it was night out, and her car would speed away. Janet would often lunge toward the door at that moment making a hideous face, blocking her nose, giving Rita the finger. Leena, she stinks. Let's have a smokola before we start. We would pull a couple of Tabs out of the refrigerator, she would turn the radio on and the Righteous Brothers would moan, *Baby Baby, I'd get down on my knees for you*. We swooned, both being in unrequited love situations. I can't remember who hers was about, she was always dumping really great guys for no good reason. Janet wasn't beautiful at all, but she had really large breasts, was small. Had beautiful skin, cool black glasses and just evoked social power in a way that made everyone want Janet to be on their side. She was smart enough, she wasn't ambitious. She liked to laugh at people, to lounge. I always knew she was curious about me, had an admiration of sorts, and it caused her to invite me into an intimacy that was about sharing her most vulnerable feelings. The social application of this bond was kind of scary. It was kind of like she would lure me into her stylish circle of girls, and then when the whim would strike her in the schoolyard she would turn on some aspect of my existence, my messy hair, a new pimple, the disarray of my rolled-up pleated skirt, the possibility that I was getting fat. I think I radiated hurt me when we were at school. She was always trying to make a circle around herself and the only way she could define its edges was to have someone to tug in and out, depending on whether that particular Wednesday she thought I was cool.

I had my own version of this dance. Sometimes I could feel the danger coming. It was a slow day in school, nothing funny had happened. And nothing had happened last night, it wasn't close to the weekend, there was no need to make plans, talk about clothes, about borrowing them from one another or going shopping. There'd be a lull. I would break into song. Not my own voice, but some parody of a heartbroken girlish girl on the radio. I would mess my hair up even more. I loved to perform. Here it protected me. As well as being Janet's scapegoat, I was Janet's clown. There was a whole world of outside images to attack, beyond our momentary arrangements of cool. We were borderline working class/middle class. Our school was confused, being merely Catholic, not being utterly elite, but enough wealthy families allowed their children to attend Arlington Catholic because it was a new high school built with the funds from St. Agnes parish, so it behooved the parents who attended the church and had supported it for decades to send their children to this basically free private school. There were poor kids at Arlington Catholic as well. I think in our circle I was the poorest. But I was smart and was very well acquainted with music and was funny. And Janet was teaching me to dress. Or keeping me away from looking really bad. She was kind of a tough mom. Who we didn't include in our group were rats. That's what we called the people who wouldn't go to college, who were essentially breeders, not "Harvs." Which was us—kids who hung out at Harvard Square, who were cool.

Just a few years ago we had all been rats. It was the defining look of junior high. Tight little scarves, teased hair, pointed boots. But somehow the transition from grade school to high school had weeded the rat look out. The only way we could articulate this transition was mockery, which was where I came in. I pulled my skirt up even higher like a rat. I threw my blazer back, exposing my shoulders. "Uh felt so helpless, what could I do." Sometimes Janet would chime in, *do-do*. "Remembering all the things we'd been through."

Suddenly there'd be a circle around me in the black tar schoolyard surrounded by a chain link fence which faced an immense parking lot, and beyond that the Telephone Company where my friend's mother worked and sometimes I paid my family's bills. "Remember," (Janet would whisper "walking in the rain"). "Remember..." I drew all my energy up for the crescendo of the song. I had a great voice. I felt it. "What ever happened to, the boy that I once knew. The boy who said, he'd be truuuuuuuuuue?" At that moment I had enormous black hair, a black leather jacket, great legs, was so tall.

The day around me was pearly grey, I felt sweat rising to the surface of my skin with this tingling. "Leena," said Susie, breathless. Quietly charmed. I had one kind of power—art, an occasional spectacle. Other than through punishment, it was how I paid my dues. My pain made me sing.

I definitely know who the boy was I was crying about in the kitchen. And like the one in the song, he's already dead. His name was Ohzie. Everyone had a nickname in our culture. I think it was an Irish thing. To tack on a little "ee" sound at the end of people's names. It was a dedicatedly cute, familiar reality. Mike O'Hara, Ohzie, was this guy who had a chipped front tooth, and the part that was knocked off had been glued back on, and now he had a little yellow line running through the corner of this re-assembled tooth. There was something greyish about his brown hair, dull colored. He had a grey-blue Valiant and he went to the public school, Arlington High, not ours. He hung out with a gang of collegiate jocks. They were hockey players.

In the beginning of my sophomore year the junior girls, who were

Ohzie's age, who were always watching us, had become interested in our existence because of the flattering light that came our way because of Janet's brother, and so these girls accepted me in stages.

First they allowed the information to come my way that they thought I was cute. This was exciting to me. One of them, Sandy Neilon, was a crush. I apply these terms now. I would see these older girls who were junior cheerleaders and I would watch them during games and I decided Sandy was mine. I loved her. She had long brown hair, big lips, and freckles. Many light brown freckles. Once I even dreamed of making out with her. I woke up happy. Janet informed me that Sandy Neilon thought I was cute. It made school dances erotic, dressing for Sandy. I don't remember her having a boyfriend. I remember her having just broken up with someone. I liked her being alone, but having the aura of sex. Her name, Neilon, made me think of (her) legs. She had a moment of great beauty in her junior year and by senior year she had gained weight and got a bad haircut. But there was just this light.

So first I learned that she liked me and the next news was that Ohzie did. There was this kind of girl love where the older girls pick their favorites from the younger girls and then they find an outlet for this love, a guy. They direct a guy towards their girl. It was a way of conferring status. He had a car. One day he was leaning against a wall near Brighams and we must have been waiting to do something because the boys started to go away and then the girls and him and I stayed and stayed and then he said, want to go have a cigarette? I loved that he smoked. None of those athletic guys smoked. I got into his car and we rode around. One of the things my job at Shore's did was pay for cigarettes. We did this a bunch of times. I don't remember making out with him at all. He was slow. It was a joke about him. There was something really spacy about Ohzie. I thought about it when he died of an aneurysm in his twenties. That maybe there had been this pressure on his brain all along. Then one Sunday night after a hockey game he asked me if I wanted to go to a party with George and Sherry. They were this couple we always used to laugh at at dances. They danced completely wrapped around each other like adults. Just grinding away.

They just both had adult sexualities already. George was a short guy with a rough complexion, but handsome in that military kind of way. His father was a retired General or something and he ran his family like a platoon, and was really violent and scary with his sons. George was a small football player. Sherry had piles of dark hair, was really smart, had large breasts a great body, was such a good dancer (in kind of a rat way, but she was so powerful that it even enhanced her aura) and was the scariest fiercest girl on the basketball team. She would get in such fights. She would get all red. She was so serious and they were such a serious couple. I couldn't believe I was having the opportunity to hang out with them. Without even thinking about it you felt their sex. Anyway, we went to a party and we went to another party and it was dark and Sunday night and it was about nine o'clock and I never called my mother because I knew she would say no to all of this and it was my big chance. I finally came home around ten. Where were you. It was like she was going to beat me, I was a slut, really bad. You have to understand that my father was dead and the main terror in my house was that of causing my mother to feel anything because we felt so bad for her. She was alone and we had to be good.

So after that I couldn't go out after school. I was grounded for two weeks. I couldn't go out at all. I was afraid to tell Ohzie. I just didn't talk to him. I couldn't tell him that I had to stay in. I was ashamed that I wasn't allowed to go out. That it had been a problem. I didn't know how to explain it. And my mother never paid any attention to me. Punishing me was the only time she did. So I'd go shopping with her after school. I would eat and eat. I remember her watching me make an immense angel cake and peaches and ice cream thing in a cereal bowl and her flirting with me in a musical voice, "You'll be sorry." She told me that she gained a lot of weight around my age and she didn't want to see that happen to me. When I finally got out I went to a party and Ohzie was standing there leaning against a wall. I thought he was going to talk to me but he never came over. One of the junior girls told me he was waiting for me. Wasn't he the man. That was the end of it. Ohzie was what I was singing about in the kitchen while the Righteous Brothers wailed. It would have led to sex, I think. He was perfect. He had cigarettes and a car.

# 15.

On Saturday mornings I had to bring them eggs. Mostly they had poached eggs on toast. That was normal. Some of them had a little soft boiled egg in an egg cup. Many of them had special egg cups. It was like they had them all my life. "I see you've brought me my soft boiled egg," said Mrs. Curtis, who was really nice for a while. You'd watch their personalities drop right out. One day Mrs. Curtis would be a nice old woman with a sweetness about her and an intelligent gleam in her eye. Yes, I like my egg very much. Started to stare a little too long after she said that. You'd watch the skin pucker and start to grow slack. Greyen. You'd watch the eyes get tiny, go away. First the nurses would encourage her to eat. Then you'd see them feed her. I was always afraid they'd ask me to feed her, and one day they did. I pushed the little spoon against her silent lips. The eyes looked scared. Who am I? Like a little cat. I'd see her whiskers glow in the morning light. I'd just sit there for a while. Push the spoon against her lips. Let them get a little yolky. I'd sit there in the light just like her. You're not too good at that, said Lois, for once being nice.

Mr. Casey had a big plate of fried eggs. Three of them. He was bald. And had a voice like he was from some other part of the country. The Midwest. It wasn't the voice so much, it was the words and how he'd say them. Well, young lady, how are you? Huge teeth, dentures I think. He was bald and wore big glasses and had a loud salesman voice. But he was mostly gone. Greeting me was the one thing left he could do. And eat his eggs. Feed himself. He seemed to read the newspaper. It was always there with his glasses when he didn't have them on. They would just rest there on the counter. On the lap of his table. Their furniture was so funny, if you thought of it apart from them. It was someplace between school desks and adult high chairs.

Some of them had these formica pieces that would swing around the front of their beds so they could sit up. Some of them had flaps like that attached to their sitting chairs. They were there to sit, to eat their last meals, and then to lie down. If Mr. Casey wasn't sitting there with the big eggs in front of him he was just standing there in his room like a burst of energy that hadn't yet left. He was tall, had a big wiry build. But he reminded me of this horrible character on Superman. It was someone really evil and finally at the end of the episode his face was in the sky. This huge bald man. Still talking. Scaring Superman. It was like he had taken over the skies. He was mad. This is what Mr. Casey really felt like. A nightmare sun. And when he wasn't thinking, when he wasn't even waiting at all he would still stand there like a plant in his brown and maroon wool striped bathrobe with his slippers on going 'smack, smack.' It sounded like lips but it was his moist jaws creaking, his loose shaky teeth. It was his gears. Hello young lady how are you. Smack smack. It affected me so much. I could hear it when my back turned. It felt sexual. Appreciative. I'd like to eat you up. Smack. He turned up in my dreams. There was a burning sky, the world had ended and Mr. Casey had a huge ladle and was in charge of the stew. There it was, giant tubs. One vat had human livers, one was kidneys, with barley or little tiny organs, glands, something small, white and peanut-like, tiny balls of fat sitting on the surface of the immense stew at the end of the world. All the colors were red and orange and everything was warm, too warm. He was standing there with all the parts, and he wanted you. He wanted you to become part of his soup. Smack smack. Everything was gone and there was that sound. Monster. Old monster.

One day old Hoppy was lying there still on her bed. She was beige grey. Her mouth was open. She was dead. This was bound to happen to someone. It was just a question of time. I had brought her eggs in. I put them on the little white table next to her bed with tiny silver dots. I didn't care. I stood there staring for a moment. She looked like a photograph of a dead pope. I had seen dead people before. I had seen plenty of them. And they were usually old. But her mouth was open like a fish. It was stiff. Her last little sniff of air had come and gone. Miss Fish, I thought. I had to come in and find her. It was just my time. Lois, I called for the nurse. It's Hoppy, I think she's dead. I was holding the tray. Um-hum. Send her eggs back down. That seemed particularly lonely. Hoppy's eggs going downstairs. Creak creak. The red light went out.

I told Janet after the weekend. Hoppy's dead. Shhitt, Leena. Janet sat down. You mean, *you know them and I know them, we both know them.* We always did Hoppy's lines. Janet started crying. It sort of made me sick. Yeah, I scratched the back of my head and I lit a cigarette. I could handle upstairs.

Mrs. Wilson cried. My, My, My, Ba-by, Ba-by, Ba-by. Her *my* sometimes would go higher and higher, my-yeeeeeeee, Baby, Baby, Baby. A picture was created of a burning house and a child that had died and I wanted there to be a story attached to her song. Her eyes were closed, usually, she had pure white hair, curly and wild with a yellow aftertone. There was a deep purple surrounding her eyes. She wore a little pink sweater. And she sang all day long. It drove everyone crazy. The nurse would jam a tray onto a shelf and mutter to her self, her teeth gritted, "Will you shut the fuck up." Everyone imitated her. You couldn't be on that floor or the one beneath it without picking it up at some point and you knew everyone went home to their families and sang Mrs. Wilson's song. Do you think something happened to her, I asked Lois. Absolutely not. She has a lovely family. She had a lovely life. She's just nuts. Finally she stopped making sounds at all and quietly died. We all wanted her little squeal to come back, just once. There's an idea that what you get in nursing homes is care and privacy. I mean, they cost a lot of money and you don't die alone. But it's sort of like being in a museum. A college dorm, a fraternity house, with old wood and stairs and a small population of people get to watch you go down. You're a stranger, an oddity. You've kind of been installed. The times when they got visitors seemed really pathetic to me. The little girls twirling in the halls. Go in and say hi to Grandma. The cards would pile up around their trays. My niece gave me this, said someone pointing to a pin on her sweater. She'd smile and you'd smile and say, oh that's nice. A person was turned into a greeting card. It wasn't like you had to send your aunt a thank you note for the check. You'd visit. She was a little bag of money sitting on a chair, smiling. Everybody had to come and see that their money was still there. I think the state paid for some people but no one ever came to see them, and they seemed almost better. The place was more intense for them. It was one world. The nurses, the trays, me, the weather, the other oddball in the room. She makes me crazy, can't you make her shut up? She never wants to talk. People with visitors were a little smug. I knew what their life was like. I think being with a person is better than caring about them. I cared about them more than their relatives did, and I didn't care about them at all.

# 16.

My friend Lorraine lived on Swan Street, which ran right into mine, Swan Place. Her house was huge and grey. There were two sides to it, two separate doors with separate numbers, 5 and 7. There were little wicker baskets next to each doorbell, I think for the mail. There were big metal knockers on the door, but to use them was a joke. You could just walk in. Hello, you'd yell into the dark house.

Once when I was exactly four years old my mother was having my sister or had already had her, I don't know. It was in the wonderful years, the end of them, before I went to school, when I had my mother alone. We were in our house and suddenly some men came in, firemen, dressed in black with their cowboy hats on and they put my mother on a chair and carried her downstairs. I felt naked and alone. I felt the hugeness of my house. I was small. There was this furniture. Curtains rugs and stuff. It's been insisted for years that my mother must have explained that this was going to happen. She would not have just left me like that. But I remember it. The huge gonging silence. And then the doorbell rang and it was the happy voice of Germaine Guyash, Mrs. Fleming, Lorraine's Mom. She lived in the huge grey house on Swan Street. There was a teeny little moment that permanently lives in my head that oh, it's okay. She will be my Mom now. It didn't seem to matter who held the job. A happy woman came. She sat in the kitchen of the grey house all day long, nervously smoking cigarettes. Years later I learned she did drugs. Happy ones that keep you busy. She came from a huge family in Ontario. She was very very poor, she had a twin. And that was exciting, that there were two of them. It seemed a string of Moms could wrap around the world with this woman's kindness and energy. It was a dark huge old house. They owned both sides and all the rooms. The Flemings took in boarders. They had all these ladies who lived in rooms. A whole life lived in a little bedroom upstairs in the Flemings' house. All of them came down, from time to time. They would sit around the metal kitchen table with Mrs. Fleming. They would all make their entrances in the doorway to the kitchen. Behind them was the dark that I continually mention. Above the dark was a wooden staircase that led upstairs, around and around. One floor was Lorraine and Bill's rooms and later on little Eileen. Beyond them lived the boarders and in all the rooms on the other side. It seemed like the Flemings had an endless number of rooms, Lorraine was always showing me another one, sometimes empty, where we could play.

But these older women, women alone in their forties and fifties and sixties, had rooms full of beads and old clothes and pictures of men. I never saw rooms like this again till years later in San Francisco, hotels on Castro full of queens. It was like old starlets lived here. But the one I mean to focus on is Mrs. Beatty.

Not Aunt Louise who disgusted me and ruined the table. Who didn't know how to make an entrance. Who just walked in with her tiny tiny steps. A gigantic head on such a small woman on such an presumptuous power trip. Very big smile when she came in, as if she had already been there and she just noticed you, and *what* are you saying now? With her very Eleanor Roosevelt no-chin look and small tan spots and many small bumps all over her face. What is that? I asked Lorraine. That's just how she looks. And wouldn't pursue it with me. I think she wore pearls, occasionally.

Or Aunt Kitty who was Lorraine's best friend and they had spent hours together in Kitty's small room, and these days were fondly referred to during me and Lorraine's early maturity once Kitty was back into business and opened a shop—a tearoom inside of an office building in downtown Boston, and Kitty read tea-leaves and her partner was an artist, a cartoonist, and she did exaggerated caricatures of their customers and then pasted their mugs all over the tearoom which was a hangout for old ladies.

Eileen draws, Lorraine would tell them, but I didn't think *this* was what I was planning to do. And Lorraine and Kitty would sing the little songs that they had sung together in Kitty's small room and I wondered how I could have missed that this was going on and it explained perhaps why in her childhood Lorraine was adverse to going out. She had a private life with Kitty in her room. No, I never saw Kitty in that house. She had shimmering silver grey hair and you knew when she was younger she had been very pretty. She had those kind of eyes. A pleased little cat, and very wry. Kitty was an exception; she moved on. Kind of show business odd, but still she was a woman and the whole gang spooked me because they were all women and women wind up in little rooms, women wind up alone.

Looking back it was not a bad scene. The final one before the Nursing Home. Many long hours in that house, and they made tea and really appreciated donuts and little sweets. And then Mrs. Beatty came in. Though she was a woman, she seemed like a man. She had chestnut brown hair piled up in turban-like folds and on top of it all she wore a little velvet hat with a veil. She wore rimless glasses with a string hanging from their legs. She sometimes smoked a cigarette in a holder. And she had faded freckles all over her face. Her voice. That was the most prominent thing about Mrs. Beatty. She had a scratchy gravelly voice that always seemed on the verge of making a tremendous joke. She was jeering at someone and yet you could see she was smiling, she was joyful and her joy had a foreign air of sophistication. She wore a big brown fur coat. With fox heads in there somewhere. I remember her wearing navy blue. The dress under everything, perhaps. She came from the beginning of the century, the 20s or the 30s. She was like Arthur Godfrey, or especially, Franklin Delano Roosevelt. Though he was never my president, but my parents', I knew Franklin Delano

Roosevelt, and he was on teevee in history shows. He smoked like her and wore those glasses and had that twang. So she was left from his time. I had been in her room because Lorraine did little errands for all these women, and once I had suggested that I could do it too but she said her mother wouldn't like it, and besides they were her friends. And they were. Lorraine had a ton of old tired mothers who loved her. In Mrs. Beatty's room there were a lot of pictures of one handsome young man with his hair slicked back and parted down the middle. Many of the frames were round and the photographs were brown, which I had never seen before. And she had great curtains in her room, very curly and fancy and her bed had the most complicated spread and there were little round tables and chairs and more than anyone's room hers was a world. There was an overhanging lamp which I think was blue, blue and white. It was like she was royalty. It was like she was a queen. And of all the women who lived in the house Mrs. Beatty made the best entrances. In fact she made only entrances. She would arrive and hover framed in the doorway to the kitchen not saying a word, and Mrs. Fleming (known in particular to Mrs. Beatty as Gerry) would look up as if surprised and go *Mrs. Beatty*, as if she was deeply honored and kidding at the same time, and Mrs. Beatty would light up and say something in her growling flirting voice to Gerry, and then she had arrived. She would never sit down, she never joined the crew in the kitchen. She had her moment and then she was gone. Her moment was long. She introduced the concept of boarders to me. I asked Lorraine who Mrs. Beatty was one day when I was very young, and Lorraine said she is one of our boarders. And then I had a category for them all. I never wanted to be a woman because they wind up alone.

So when I saw Mrs. Beatty's big bare butt being lifted off a potty seat by a nurse who was strong enough for that, and I could smell her shit, but mostly it was her white nakedness and the fact that Mrs. Beatty was one of the most covered people I had ever seen in my life, certainly the most covered woman, and there she was without her hat or her cane which I had forgotten, which added to her elegant authority, and it was all gone, her colors and her fur and even her voice. I don't even remember quiet whimpers from this white marvel arched over her pan after taking a dump. The hair was all hanging down loose, there was so much of it, and she turned or I saw her face somehow and there was nothing in it. She was gone. I almost convinced myself it was not her. I wanted it to be someone else so I wouldn't have to have seen what I saw. This is Mrs. Beatty, said the nurse, disgusted. And the unspoken message was she won't be here long. When did she go there? I never heard. Someplace in my life between ten and fourteen.

# 17.

I hate being a woman. I am forty-five, almost fifty. I was walking across some cement the other day, across the kiosks, going out. Rushing someplace with a cigarette in my hand. I thought of that girl. I was leaning in Soho one night, on Broadway, waiting for someone. A girl came around the corner. She had my face. She had long hair, was kind of dreaming, looking sad. She had a cigarette in her hand. She was on her own. I felt so lonely looking at that girl. Around twenty-two or twenty-five. Just moved to New York. Had an apartment. This big-faced white girl. Kind of strong. A healthy girl. But sad. She wasn't doing anything tonight. You could tell. She had her cigarette.

It was like the whole vague longing of youth was in that smoke, loosely but closely held in her fingers. What time of year was it. Maybe fall. There was fall in the air, there was her, and her cigarette. And her body. She had a walk. She was kind of drifting. She probably intended to buy some food. She was moody. Maybe she was going to her friend's apartment. It didn't matter. She could have even been going to a party. It didn't matter. Not to her. Her walk counted. The fact that she was out there alone with her thoughts. Not much had happened. It wasn't on her. She was kind of sad and kind of free.

When I was twelve, it was the last day of school and I was lying in bed and something felt wet underneath me and I felt weirdly sick. I got up and there was blood underneath me and I faintly understood and I pulled myself up, I remember cotton around me, pajamas, and my sheets and I carried myself downstairs, my bare feet hitting the fake wool of the carpet and I can hear those dull thuds as I wavered down. I went into the bathroom and sat on the toilet and there was more of it, blood, and there was this whirring feeling inside of me. I thought I was going to pass out and I did. There were big huge clots of blood, it looked like liver, which I hate, pouring out of this thing I wouldn't yet call cunt or anything. I didn't know about the inside of me. I was afraid to break myself. I knew there was an up, but I didn't go there. I thought I would get hurt. It was almost like I was already broken, somehow. I got up from the toilet and opened the door not even flushing I think. And I fell down in the doorway. Completely blacked out and collapsed. My brother came running. Mom, Eileen fell down. Oh are you alright? I guess she got a look at the toilet. C'mon. You'll be alright. She pulled me up. Later I got one of those huge cotton pads to put between my legs and one of those obscene stretchy bands that have little hooks with claws through which you attach the thinner, almost gauzy part of the giant pad. It's all closed up. And you flood one and you change it. I really bleed a lot.

Years of it. Being a woman. I was a woman before, I suppose. Bleeding through my uniform in school. Blood on my seat. Just blatantly announcing to the world I was female. Excessively so, and I had been a boy so long. Somehow my periods would have to be the worst. I remember some girls referred to it as their friend. It seemed to suit the weird advertising Kotex used. Soft medium range colors. The white product filling the inside. Later Tampax with that typeface that seemed Japanese. Do they print the boxes in Japan? Nothing in America is ever printed in that strange mechanical slightly Asian type. Where did that come from. Now I could get pregnant.

I think I'm lucky these days when I haven't stained the bed. I remain profuse, a bad visitor. Always washing out someone else's sheets. My blood has the same drama now that it did was when I was a kid. What I mean is that it begins in kind of a flood and it goes out that way. I mean I could probably bleed for five more years. I've never had a baby.

Never really considered except for one afternoon on a raft in a pond in New Hampshire. Everything was surrounded by light, the strangeness of that thought. I could have a kid. And it passed like a cloud in the sky. But I feel my body remembering itself, now when I feel that sickening pleasure of blood. It's got to be different for us. I'm imagining every woman I know spending 24, 25 hundred days in her life with blood pouring out of the inside of her body announcing her ability to lay an egg. All that blood like some kind of sex with yourself. Is it clotty. Is it red, brown; does it look too bright. Don't you think better when you're bleeding, don't you want to stay home and smoke and read and write. Don't you feel tremendously sexy. Have you spent years hiding it, arming yourself against revelation, the stains and the bloody smell. Do you want to fuck. I remember my friend describing his face when he described eating the pussy of a bleeding woman. That he had red wings.

I was walking across the cement with my smoke. It floods when it begins and it floods when it goes. You start to go crazy. I know I do. The whole world become my enemy. I cry for myself. All alone. A life ruined. Tragic mistakes, things I repeat again and again in my head, trying to get right. Sometimes I can taste the thought of the thing I should have said, should have done. I'm so ashamed of myself. Bragging, raging, remaining quiet. Everyone I talk to has that edge in their voice. They pity me. I'm over. You can see it in my eyes. And you must leave me forever. I can never forget what you've done. I didn't deserve this. I don't love you anymore. You had my body. I was completely open to you. It's taken me years to get this way. No one could touch me. They couldn't get through. I gave you such a gift. My cunt. And now we're through. And then I bleed. I wonder if that girl had blood on her jeans. They were dark.

# 18.

Janet quit the job before I did. She turned 16, she got a job at Sears. I was alone. I began working with a big girl, Kathy Kelly, the daughter of one of the nurses. Mrs. Kelly was a skinny little tough woman. She smoked cigarettes, had jet-black hair that she must have dyed by then. I'm beginning to understand the meaning of female hair color. When you lose that, everything changes. It's like you're going bald. Your hair's getting lighter people say.

Mrs. Kelly didn't like me. I felt. I was afraid of her. Some people, you know their criterion for life is, are you tough? They sniff you out. They decide to treat you a certain way, based on that whiff. They might need to wipe you out. I was embarrassed by my desire to get Mrs. Kelly to like me. I'd say something mean about someone. Trying her out. She ignored me. I just had to work hard and shut up. Which was probably her thing, getting that.

So Kathy had the job. She was big and sexy. Tall, large breasts, hair piled up in that greaser way. Tight uniforms. Little shoes. Little feet, really, which was hot. Smoked, of course. She slammed her trays around at night. I took tips from her as to when we could smoke. She controlled the radio, singing along and no choruses from me, thank you. You go to the Catholic school, she asked once. Then her mother would come down. She would sit there in her chair looking skinny and tired and old. She'd look at me then because she needed someone at whom to aim a tiny groan the moment before she lit her cigarette. It was a bitter world. She had a son who was in Vietnam who she was clearly crazy about. He married a gook. He sends me a picture of this chink. What am I suppose to say. She's a chink. Ah, she shrugs and cringes. He loves her. Great, I say. She looks like a girl for a moment. You two sweethearts almost done? I'll finish my smoke outside. Wait for John. The other son.

Everything shifted a tiny bit. Janet was gone, Kathy hated me, Mrs. Kelly was waiting and Mrs. Shore started to end her night, because everyone was down there, with a beer. Some bottled beer, something special that came in heavy green bottles. I think it was German or Dutch. It being European made it seem medicinal. And Mrs. Shore was clearly sick, I think it was alcoholism. So she'd pour her beer in a very solid looking glass and she'd place the full glass behind me where I was setting up trays. On this little table. I don't know why she put it there, there was plenty of room in the kitchen. So the heat was on one night. It seemed I was going particularly slow. Maybe it was the holidays, a special meal. I was depressed. Janet being gone it was like being alone. Smash, smash, I was slamming my trays down, trying to go fast, trying to let them know I was working hard. It was just a job. It used to be our secret. Crash. I don't know what I was thinking about but I could feel them all watching me so I quickly turned and knocked Mrs. Shore's beer off the table, onto the floor spilling it halfway across the room and breaking her glass. You, she stared and pointed at me, you get out of here and never come back. It was like I was a dog. Mrs. Kelly smiled. It was my first job. And I cried when I was walking home in the dark, so relieved.

# 19.

Mike and I were in Harvard Square down in the basement of one of those wooden pub places—you know, little brown ceramic tubs of cheese to put on crackers. Very cheddary. The lighting was kind of nice, warm, and things were feeling okay. Mike worked at Jordan's, I was at Filene's. I'd meet him outside the Chauncy St. exit of Jordan's. It was a really crummy place. This dark horrible escalator. Mike couldn't stand me. For being there, for waiting for him. I had never had a boyfriend before. I was supposed to be there. I worked right across the street and we lived in the same town and took public transportation. Where was I supposed to go. He was a miserable guy. Had a little cold sore tonight. He put Blistex on it like an old man. Just unbelievably anxious. We headed to Harvard Square. In complete silence. I wanted to scream. Nothing worse than being quiet with a man. Holding on to our cold little poles on the subway. Few pops? He said abruptly when we got to the Square. I actually had a ton of reading to do, but the words would not come out of my throat. Just nodded. So we went to that place. I wanted to get the first Heineken down. Ah. Feeling better. He smiled at me now. We were doing a crossword puzzle. There was always something, some little game. What's a slang word for a good boy? Pi. *Pi*, he laughed. I think so. Pi. He looked down smiling. A few beers in I began talking about my mother. I had at least four beers. Why was I thinking about her? They both ignored me. I wanted to go home. I was drinking, so it was impossible. It was a sad attachment I was watering. "I really love my mother." Mike smiled. No, I do.

She is absolutely great. I don't think she's so great. What, she gave you a beer. I like your mother alright. No, you don't. What do you mean, she's not so great. I don't know your mother at all. She's great. Leena, I think *you're* really drunk. I love her.

The day I realized I could bring her flowers was a happy one. Neither my brother or sister would ever think of that. A bunch of roses. I got them in the subway. Why thank you, she said. I wanted to be the beloved son. I bought her a London Fog raincoat. I stole money out of my register at the Coop to buy it. Powder Blue. I bet she still owns it. I bought her an Etienne wallet. The most elite brands to my knowledge. I wanted to shower my mother with hopefulness. For the future. I wanted her to feel safe. I was a good son. I was not a problem. She didn't worry about me. I was never inside too much.

The world would always take care of Eileen. My brother and sister were the unhappy children. What are we going to do about them? It bubbled up like a ancient spring, this love for my mom, the perfect woman. I was nineteen, maybe twenty. Want to get going, Leena? We were both really bombed. Making out on the back of the bus. Grabbing his dick. It was cold. The cold bus. Who do they think we are, the riders? They had designed a cold plastic can for the people of Boston to ride in. Neon orange, like that would warm us up. We *were* warm, with his black wool topcoat, tweed, and I had tights. I was the sexual aggressor in public. I was really drunk. Do you want to come up? Come on. Sounds of two drunken, waddling humans. We scraped against the wall. We hissed.

We stumbled through the den, we walked into the kitchen. I turned the light on. I had lived in this house since I was three. I knew where everything went, I knew the effect of every possible action inside of this place because the heart of the machine, my mother, reacted the instant anything was moved. She let us know how each part affected every other part. So for instance I knew, though she was not responding at the moment, that the neon light in the kitchen was shining right into my mother's eyes as she lay in her bed right around around the corner. I was engaged in the deepest taboo. You didn't have people inside my house. Not much. And when you did, it wasn't fun. Which added to the obscenity of dating. A house essentially closed to the world was being entered by a man who was fucking me. This was roughly the impact of any guy who walked in the door. The total queerness of the situation was more than anybody should bear. Though my mother was Polish, the feeling was Irish. I guess it was Catholic. Or just us. I didn't fight my mother. I did what I was told and the rest I hid. I had no confrontations with her. We just kind of brushed right past each other in a romantic state of detestation—for being women.


My mother is a big-shouldered broad. I don't know why I say it that way, but one of my favorite photographs of my mother has me standing with a little bit of sunlight spilling on my baby legs, and I'm in a bathing suit on a porch somewhere, probably Marshfield, and behind me are three women, my mother, Aunt Anne, and Nonie. All these women have gone on to their separate fates, even my mother who's still alive. I feel like I'm part of her destiny now. I hold my floppy hat, a large woman's hat aloft, I hold the brim of the hat like wings and I am playing, I am taking off. The women behind me look grand. My mother does. She is a knockout in this picture. Because she has big shoulders. Because she looks strong. Because she's trim. Her hair's wrapped in some kind of turban. She has kind of a crooked smile, almost a swagger. I think my dad's taking the picture, and I think he modeled my mother a lot. She's a very malleable woman, despite her strong appearance, and he liked women of the Barbara Stanwyck school. He was a dashing man himself. There is hardly any femininity in my family. We are weak people, we are not striving people, we are not brave people, but we are posturing people, and we are masculine. We like the weapons of our time: the clothes, the belts, the boots, the hats, the lifted legs, leaning on cars. We like to look great. When we do, we know "I am." It's an adolescent kind of power—it reigns in the world of photographs, of moments triumphed over in a flash of appeal.

My father, though shy, was a truly convivial man. Professional actors are horrible people, everyone knows that. But one need only go to a memorial service to understand that every life is an act. The more people you have involved, the bigger an actor you are. My father was a small actor. His life was a stunning bit part. One of the features of his role was to frame my family in its moments of torture and beauty. Long after his death, I realize that more than anything, the man had an eye. He framed his woman, my mother, one sunny afternoon, in a shot with the other broads. I don't know why I'm using that word. I guess he framed me. His baby daughter twirling around in a huge floppy hat. The eternity of his wife, the idea of woman crowding the frame was so perfect and immense that day. It was my mother's body, her bones, her perfect joy in being alive in her thirties and looking great in her husband's eyes as he smiled and took a picture of her with her sister, her daughter and her friend.

Leena, are you sure this is okay? She's asleep, don't worry. I bet he didn't even realize where my mother's bedroom was. In this small apartment in a two-family house which we owned, life was as fixed as the stations of the cross. Moments of which we were never to be deprived: my mother watching teevee, my mother eating. My love for her was a damp piece of laundry, wrung out for years, twisted by hand. *Flap, squirt.*

Three memories of my mother: the medal she wore around her neck, something holy and ornate. Warm and swinging towards me as she kissed me goodnight. I wanted her but I hated that thing. It was a warm demon head, a piece of metal—a monstrance. She had a metal button box next to her bed. A black oval-shaped box with flowers on it. It had a pair of handles that you could flip down. Pull off the lid. Shimmering gold inside. Every button in the world. Ones from old coats, ropy ones. Little silver buttons, or fat ones like berries. Endless tiny white buttons, all sizes. Before an old shirt would leave us, my mother would snip off the buttons. Clink! It was the goodbye hall of all our clothes. There were dead people in there too. You could shake the box and they'd go dancing around. Ker-clang, Ker-clang, Ker-clang. A lonely, shattered sound. It was wildly musical. An animal or an accident. The old thing scared me. It sat on a shelf in the small table next to my mother's bed. My sister loved to dump the buttons all over the place, to lie on her bedspread. You'd get that smell. A cake, a fruit-cake is what originally came in this box and you'd smell this sweet old food while dozens of buttons were strewn across the folds of my mother's bed. It was that smell. Buttons and food. It felt like a witch thing. I had to stop it. Too much death. It was just too much for me.

It became a joke in my family. Nyaah! the button box, and my brother and sister would shake it near my head, at my bedroom door. I stood there, panting and wheezing, gasping with tears as I held the old chipped door shut with my weight and my outside foot, safe for a moment in my room.

They attacked me because I was strong and this was so freaky. I stood tall and normal like my mother. Though it was her box, her invention. And it was from her room, this hideous trap.

If I talk about my mother, I'm talking about a view. Her legs and the steam. She was ironing up there, I was lying on the floor seeing how far I could stretch my arms and legs out. I was a star. It was our quiet little day. When I looked down Swan Place, standing on a chair, and saw the green trees in early spring and there's globs of lilacs in each rounded form of tree jutting up into the sky, nearly crossing the telephone wires—in a storm how they sway from left and right. All that, the leafy scenery, I think is her. I'm standing still and a woman is down in front of me on her knees. She's made an Easter coat for me out of my uncle's sailor uniform. She has pins in her mouth, it looks funny.

I saw a woman sewing once, in a dry cleaners in New York and she looked Polish—the pins in her mouth, I got dizzy. The old world, the past washed up too quick. She's washing my hair and I'm screaming. I'm crying out loud. It's really hot. She's says my father's going to hear me at work, I'm screaming so loud. I wonder if it's true. I forget to ask him. It is so hot. And when she makes braids she tugs my head so hard.

We go to Grant's and buy a quarter yard or more of those plaid ties I wear on each tail like a horse. I choose a plaid I like. In the school picture I wear them and I look very serious. A thinking girl.

She's asleep. Do you want a beer, or don't you? Pushing myself into him. In the kitchen with the neon lights of my childhood jamming my drunkenness to an incredible high. I would like it if he would eat my pussy in the kitchen.

It seemed too late for everything. C'mon, c'mon. I was totally alone. My enemy breathing, asleep in her bed. It was sudsy darkness, the parlor. Bringing him down on the scratchy couch. We had fucked here before. The silent ticking of the house. My mother's breathing. Slam. The day is gone. I mean, it's off and running, open. In all the places in the world, under bleachers, along the grey pond. We woke up on the couch in my mother's house. I had on the itchiest grey miniskirt she had shortened for me on her sewing machine. It was around 11AM. She had gone to work. The skirt sort of around my hips, like a ruffle. Mike, still yawning, moaning, leans on me, drooping over my shoulder. I could see his ass, uh oh. I guess we passed out before we got to fucking. Our weapons out. She went to work. Did she drink coffee? I looked in the sink. You know, my mother takes a good stretch, but the air smells strange. The open beers. Ions bouncing from the kitchen lights being on all night. Shit, Leena. He wakes. I'm late for work. Which was not the worst of it. Still want to go to that play? He looked at me, eyes glazed. Trying to decide if I was crazy. Sure. Slam. I'm walking around. Our beers still out. One in the kitchen. One on the floor next to the couch. Not spilled. So she had some coffee. She would not let me go. I can see it. Cup in the sink. Her house.

I forced myself to go to class. Have the day. I needed him to forgive me. No, I'm going home tonight. No beers. We had free tickets to the Schubert. These two beaky guys were struggling to the death. One guy was Chinese. The play was about socialism and poverty. And dirty violent sex. Brecht. "The Jungle of the Cities." Two men with bird masks on were dancing around the stage. They were struggling to find the power to be alive and kill. There were cardboard sets. Red and black like silent film. Harsh and cartoony. In the blackness I killed her. I'm drowning. I'm swallowed in the stillness of the Schubert Theater. Sitting with this guy who was sort of my man. Which was over. My bomb. I did it.

My mother and I...it was like we broke up. It was our lover's quarrel. At last. Slipping around each other for several days. One night I was lying in my little bed, the tiny little boat. I was constantly squirming. Thought I could somehow convince her it hadn't happened. We were not having sex. It was hot. I was thinking about it. It was was, um, a joke.

Then it cracked in the middle, rose up from the gases of Sunday. Nobody home, oh now—where's Terry. Terry, he's uh at um someone's house. Bridgid's at her friend's. I'm all alone with the Polish woman— my mother and the rugs. The sound of padded clocks. Ka-turr, Ka-turr. Everything dead. I'm slipping upstairs with a cup of tea. I'm afraid. I'm invisible. I'm not here.

It got unleashed. You have broken my heart. You tramp. The hair yanking like something from hundreds of years ago. Like a goat. My jaw slack. Insane, she hated me so much. Little bomb in the house. My sex. She shrieked, "Your father's been dead for seven years." Oowang. "And-don't-think-I-haven't-wanted-it!" She pulled my brain. My stomach dropped. Oozing up the stairs. Like a stain.

Leena, I don't know if I can handle this anymore. What do you mean, you have to come up. She hates me. I'm going down the street. I know you're meeting that monster. She calls you the monster. Leena, that's not funny. I'm so alone. Black hole I fell down every day for sex. The bloated belly from the pill so I won't get knocked up. I liked it better when I was afraid. Waiting for my period. The fear seemed like sex. Tristan and Isolde. She found the pills first. She started the story.

What was she doing in my desk? She never comes up. Now he was gone, and I moved out.

This little apartment in Boston's North End. Crying in my workshirt in my room. Really not a girl anymore. A boy on her bed in the world.

# 20.

This was such a long affair. Two years. He was married and lived near a beach with his wife. He had a kid. Since I knew right away that I would be madly in love with him, I determined to have lots of other affairs. And I did. I gave him crabs. He told me he was lying in bed with his wife and he saw one walking across his thigh. He always presented these things to me with horror as if I should be protecting his marriage. It scared me, his anger. I asked him once if his wife fooled around. She better not. He angrily puffed his cigarette. At certain moments like that he looked really conceited. It was all about him. It just didn't occur to me to challenge him about this stuff. His coldness scared me and it kept him separate which kept him hot. My brother sells wine for a living. One Christmas he gave me a case of really good wine, and that's what we'd drink for a while when Robert came over. We both smoked cigarettes. I had this gold brocade couch that you had to pull out. I had lots of records. Django Reinhardt. Jazz. Stuff that I thought was cool in college. I only had two boyfriends. Big romantic ones who were mean and really had me. Handsome men. Robert's wife was French. He was so impressed by that. She obviously knew that he screwed around. There was this painter, Greg. He would call Greg in the morning. In case his wife called or if she had already, the friend would cover his ass. Obviously, his wife had Greg's number. I liked hanging around with him and I liked having sex. I don't think I had an orgasm even once. I think that I faked it once in a while. I liked his beauty. He wasn't very versatile. I think I wanted to give him a blow job the first night and it wasn't for him. It was weird. And he didn't have a clue about eating pussy. I think it was beauty for him too. He was built very well. He was a short guy with wonderful arms, shoulders, legs, the whole bit. I just always want my lovers to be beautiful and he was. So it really seemed very infantile, fucking sure, but lying around kissing, talking, even showing him my poems in bed. I would bring out a big pile and he would tell me which ones were the good ones. It was very clear cut, and I appreciated that. I didn't really ask what was wrong with the ones he didn't like. He didn't like it if you got too personal. I think he liked metaphor. Which I don't believe in. He was a very wonderful poet, though a little light and cold. He did not write his best ones for her. There was this really bad one in which they went sailing and then went home and had sex. Ugh. He wrote a good one for me about being lazy. I was his crown of that—his idleness. But he liked being married. He didn't know where he'd be without her. He told me about love. Eros and agape. We were eros, clearly. I liked that. One of his poet friends lived around the corner from me. He called me on Christmas Day. I'd be moping at home, searching the tragedy of my life, hating my family, *unusual.*

Rejecting all invites to eat with my friends whoever they were. I liked to be alone. Maybe I had a cat. Anyway, he called. He was at Tim's. Could he come over. He was just going out for some cigarettes. It was Christmas Day. Fast sex. Sometimes he would suggest that being with him was keeping me from finding some guy. He'd ask me if I ever thought about sleeping with women. No. I just didn't like him implying that. It was none of his fucking business. No. Why do you ask. I just think you would like it. I don't know. It seems like you would try.

I organized a reading in a bar and invited him to take part. I was bombed on Jack Daniel's because the booze was free. And just the tension of organizing made it go right to my head. The nice part about having a secret boyfriend was that it didn't hold me back. He was like a part-time vice. An obsession. So I was loudly yacking to my friend about how beautiful he was while he was reading. Turns out I was sitting right next to his wife. Lights came up and he innocently introduced me to his kid who was also there. The kid clung to my finger too long. It was funny. I didn't even look at his wife. Not really. I just felt she looked like a snake. I mean, at that moment I knew she heard me.

After that incident Robert didn't call me for two weeks or a month. Then he was sniffing around. He worked in mid-town and I went and had lunch with him. We took that tram to Roosevelt Island then we took it back. We did that a few times. I remember being in the air with him. I remember him being incredibly sad because he would never travel around the world again. I think he had been in the Peace Corps or something. And believe me, in his poetry he milked it for all it was worth. I was like some foreign country he got to go to whenever he liked. I remember guys I was having sex with around that same time just going totally psychotic when we had sex, grovelling around my cunt like a dog. On the same furniture as him. Or some unlikely guy being a really great fuck. It really wasn't about sex with him. He was my last boyfriend. I kind of played he was my husband. I like a nice handsome man. A sneaky, conservative sort.

I never thought wild guys were hot. He asked me so many times if I liked women. There were two ends to our thing. Once I demanded he leave his wife and be with me. I was shutting the door. Another morning he was lying on my bed. I don't think we even bothered to have sex. I started to cry. I'm in love with Rose.

Rose was a poet, this girl we both knew. He turned away. He rolled to the other side of the bed. I liked my freedom and they could be conservative. They know where I am.

# 21.

It was pretty easy, 87 to 95, then 91 to 84, to 20 and then it was right off 20, I guess on 9. Driving along 9 I saw a diner called Edgemere and I decided that was the diner. It was closed and a man in the gas station next door said it had been there since the twenties.

Later my mother agreed that the waitress had dark hair, red lipstick and was tall. The waitress was very friendly with Nellie, knew her, and *sure*, said my mother because Nellie was there every Sunday with a different family member when the weather was bad, no picnic, and then added that she (the waitress) probably wouldn't know her (my mother) now. Was she your age? My mother paused, standing in the kitchen. I think so.

I drove up and the building big and yellow looked so familiar. And I've looked at it in lots of photographs—black and white, so finally the color is back. I'm standing in the world with the yellow building. I looked over the mound of grass that was so familiar and smaller of course than I remember from forty years ago, when I was five. A bunch of yellow tulips waving in the breeze, I remembered more of them, a flood of tulips, but just that they were there, exactly where they were supposed to be, was astonishing.

I wandered further across the grounds with my dog, and this all seemed familiar too, the endless expanse of green. I felt a tugging kind of permission, like a child inside me was shocked that I was daring to go so far from the car, but I wasn't going far and the car was mine. And there seemed to be more parking than I remember—a river of tar and cars had been popped into the midst of the endless green. There should be water right over there and there was, and I kept walking towards its rainy day whiteness. Several doughy looking brown creatures, moles, moved across the grass, kind of scurried, but too fucking slow. I saw them before Rosie did and my dog went right at them. I watched her catch one—and I hardly ever see her catch anything. I've become convinced she's unable to catch but likes to chase—she chokes at the moment of attack. I've thought she was like me, but no, she grabbed a big doughy one and shook it and threw it down and went after another and shook it again and again, holding it in her mouth. I walked over to the first and it was clearly dead, its little head flung back and its useless teeth bared. Rosie was having a hell of a time with the new one, clearly already dead, and she tore it in half and carried the remainder about with her, spraying guts everywhere. At one point I saw a pink cord which I thought of as its spine, its elastic, whatever longitudinal binding holds it together lying solo on the lawn. I thought I should stop her—*Rosie!*

She would pause for a moment as I called her name, but the pleasure of something newly dead in her mouth had a precedence I couldn't challenge. I saw myself as a weak person calling her name standing in the grass in the middle of the huge grey day at the mental hospital. I thought maybe I could lure her into the water of the pond we were approaching because she had brownish blood spewed all over her neck and chest, and now I was only thinking of my mother, next act, after we left the hospital and it will be shock enough that I brought my dog, but she must never see her covered in blood. In fact I can't tell her about this either.

I thought about my therapist expressing surprise that my mother told my sister and me about the girls who were abused in our bedroom by their stepfather, our house's previous owner, and I realized I was also full of a desire to tell her inappropriate things, always had felt that way—that *is* my understanding of family. But maybe I can be different now, and keep the blood to myself. I also thought how the murder of the blobby animals had made this mission feel complete.

I thought about myself as one who watched a murder in quiet shock, simply reiterating my belief that Rosie is an animal and therefore has no feeling about her actions and neither do I. I strolled into the lobby of the hospital now and she waited outside. She gathered quite an amount of attention, her pained waiting face in the doorway, and that facilitated my ease in walking around looking at what the lobby held— a small museum of the history of Westborough State Hospital. I had no pen and no desire to write anything down. It was a series of documents, newsclips and photographs. They listed the institution's earlier names: Westborough State Reformatory, or was it Reform School, Westborough Insane Hospital, I liked that one the best, and the script its documents were written in was the grandest, as if it were all legal and kind of like a wedding, everything that went on there. There were charts showing how many patients came in and how they fared—was it grief, pregnancy, intemperance, a number of discrete (and not really bad-sounding) conditions that moved one through the phases of their commitment, and yet it was clear by the numbers that many people died here, like my grandmother, and beginning at the end of the 19th century, there began to be as many women as men installed. As the 20th century rolled on the number of women inside became greater and greater.

I looked at photographs of the hospital bakers in pristine hats and, of course, many many modern-looking nurses. Standing outside of rounded chambers that were for god-knows-what. Whenever I read the captions or the fine print it all seemed very innocent. There was a glass case which contained instruments, medical ones, but there were no restraining forceps, braces or whatever. No information about strange operations. I saw pictures of women dressed like cowboys singing, and the piano player had her back to us, and I assumed that the cowboys were insane and the piano player was not. I saw patients performing a tug of war one happy day on the lawn. I saw pictures of rich women in hats who had just donated money to the hospital and I wondered why. Was there someone in the family, is money always shame? I saw pictures of honored doctors who had just died, and one had been the head of the hospital for a very long time. I saw a certificate that stated the hospital was now a landmark building. I asked the woman behind glass how many people were in the hospital. She didn't know. One of the clips on the wall said that there were fifteen hundred and some odd at one point maybe in the 50s, because they all had an outing and a cookout. 207, said some voice. There are only two hundred and seven people in here now. Every clip interested me to the extent that I could determine if my grandmother was in Westborough at the time of the events described in the yellowing newspaper article. I never imagined her taking part in these events. Seeing the hospital made me recall her slow walk out the door on Sundays when we went up to get her. She was bent and laughing in some silent way. And she was coming towards us really slow and she was the heart of my family. It was the only way my father had a mother and my mother had no mother, so it seemed normal that he had an old one who lived in an institution. There was something lost in the part where she was once a mother like my mother is now, and how she became a woman who walked out slow.

Then I asked who the head of this section was. I had just been standing out in the parking lot, putting my dog in the car. She had somehow gotten into the lobby which delighted everyone, everyone loves dogs, especially where they're not allowed, and I overheard someone say that I was a social worker and this was my dog, though I may be making that up, or just rearranging. Dr. Battel. She's upstairs. I immediately thought about the name. Someone I went to grade school had that name. How would I feel if someone I went to grade school with was the Medical Director of Westborough State Hospital, which was now even interested in homeopathy, according to the information in the display cases downstairs. The secretary to Dr. Battel looked a little crazed. I wondered if she had been in the hospital. Probably not. We're in Western Mass., which has kind of a poor white trash look which I associate with the insane. A gleaming, gaunt, too-scrubbed look. Can I help you, she asked. I had a relative who was in this hospital. Forty years ago. She smiled. Do I look melancholic. Melancholy was on the chart of the mental phases.

She vanished, then Dr. Battell came out. Can we go in, I asked. I felt dissed to be discussing my grandmother from a wooden bench in the hallway. We went in. She indicated a soft, but institutional looking blue chair. I sat down. My grandmother was a resident here. She died in 1957. Dr. Battel was Pakistani. It was Dr. Patel. If you would write her name down, I can tell you if we have the records. If there is a number I can reach you at. I felt like a patient. I looked out her big office windows. Then I wrote my numbers down on her Prozac pad. The ones drug companies give doctors free. I made a joke about it. If we have the records I will let you know. Thank you. I might have even shaken her hand. I got most of the blood off Rosie. And I called my grandmother by her maiden name. I forget she's a Myles like me. Mrs. Terrance Myles. She might be listed like that, I wrote on the Prozac pad. I walked down the stairs, got in my car. Drove to Dunkin' Donuts, bought lots of drinks—coffee, juice. I was going to stay on 9, go slow, but the Mass Pike kept coming up, 90, with that hat on its Massachusetts sign that's supposed to mean pilgrim, but I think leprechaun. How many people also think that? Eventually I succumbed to the faster road, the pike. I'm sick of the resistance in my personality. My grandmother's hands were clenched, said my mother. I saw her there the first time, I guess it was in forty-six, with your father, just before my baby shower. I wore a big hat. I looked spiffy. Her hands were clenched. And when they opened them they were full of smelly old food. It was horrible in there. Like you see in the movies. People sitting on the floor. Did she have her own room. My mother was standing in the little kitchen. I grew up here. No, no, she didn't have a private room. We always went up and got her. We went to where she was. It was horrible.

Walking around Arlington later with my dog. The Protestant streets. That's how I thought about them, I can feel it now. Up the streets with older houses away from the pond. We'd go there trick-or-treating, but they only gave apples, cider. Brown stucco covered in vines. Protestant houses. They lived here a very long time. Over there. That was my church. Not St. Agnes, but my favorite. I went to their rummage sales.

Bob Holesworth, junkie son of the minister, killed himself and burned the church down. So then they built this. Looks like white plastic from a train set. Stupid ugly tower. It's Unitarian. They used to have signs outside—Emerson, and Thoreau. It's sort of corny that Bob burned it down. I remember him, tall, big lips, kind of grey. A friend of mine, Mary Hill, had a crush on him. He was smart, she said. I think he was gay. Definitely went to private school. I was this Catholic kid feeding on those sayings. I'd read what Emerson said, then I'd hop on the cemetery wall and have a Parliament. Bob was rebelling against my freedom. It was *his* cigarette. The whole fucking church.

# 22.

I was lying on a raft on a pond one summer with my lover, a woman. A young woman. We began to talk about having babies. She said if one of us was going to have a baby, it should be me, because I was older than her and ought to get to it. I was 41. I was lying on that raft with this new sense of consciousness for a very brief moment. A flash. I thought about having a baby. I could do that. It felt incredibly free. It was the purest moment of the idea, utterly new. I asked a friend of mine, my best friend, if I could have some sperm. He thought about it, and said no, as he would have a responsibility to the child, that it would conflict with his celibacy. He was a monk. Years later, well about one, I learned that my girlfriend was having an affair with a man that summer. It really chills me. The August light. All that reflection on the pond.

# 23.

There was a very particular smell to Catholic school uniforms when they were ironed. And the fabric changed over the years. At first it was heavy and shiny. Always navy blue. As I got older, it got gauzy. I think it was probably cotton at first. Later on it was synthetic. They had v-necks and a zipper on the side which, once it was open, you could pull the uniform over your head. There were darts on the top, which made it be really significant whether you had tits or not. You'd think they would have thought about that, they were so hung up on bodies, but the nuns didn't design the uniforms. Inside the little pocket on the opposite side of the zipper was an old snot rag. That's what you kept there. A flowery little girl one that stayed in there for months. We were usually allowed to begin school in real clothes, but quickly the ladies came to measure us, lift your arms. Having a stranger deal with your body. The uniform arrived in a plastic bag with some big piece of paper, light brown, explaining in numbers your length and your width. My size. Immediately I was different from my old friends. It was always going to happen. I was living in a public school neighborhood. They had stupid and strange beliefs in God. Once the Delays insisted that at the end of the world all the non-Catholics would be left on the burning planet. I had never heard of such a thing, and if I went to a school whose sole purpose was to teach us all about Catholicism, and I didn't know about this, then it couldn't be true. The entire neigh-borhood turned on me in that moment, and I was forced to go in my house. Because of what I knew. Because of my uniform. I slunk in.

Crying. I told my mother.

She was washing dishes. So often I think of my mother as only wrists. No hands. Just get back out there, she said. It was too soon. I was sobbing. I went upstairs. What would a kid on teevee do? I went into my closet. It was the worst place in the world. Where the killers hung-out. Night killers. I decided to crouch there until someone came and got me. Maybe an hour passed. My father came up. He was slowly walking upstairs. I could hear the steps creak. Only he came up like that. My mother was quicker, mad. Instantly he got down with me in the dark. The cool grey of the closet. I liked his smell. What's a matter? Like one word. He was always trying to be a comedian. Danny Kaye, Sid Caesar, anything but him. Tell them…that your grandfather was a pirate!

What? Who worked under buses? That wet and shiny man. Handing out quarters and always wore a hat? That red-faced nobody? My dad was more of a pirate. He'd put a knife between his teeth. Jean Lafitte when he got drunk. Daddy, I groaned. Let's go down to supper, he said. C'mon. *Meatballs, meatballs and spaghetti*. He just wanted me to be a kid. He made me laugh. I climbed on his back and we went downstairs. Public school had ruined his life.

Our uniforms were navy blue. Two big pleats in the front. There was a little belt around the waist. Depending on how big yours was, you could yank it up and cinch it with the belt to make it shorter. It was an eight year school so you went through probably three uniforms. You could see that some girls' uniforms were slightly different and that meant that they had sisters. You could tell by the small adjustments the company made every few years in our uniforms. Some looked really different, like no one's. It would have been sad to begin St. Agnes in my sister's uniform. I needed my own.

In third grade I think, there was an announcement over the loud speaker about uniforms. Not to the whole school, but just the third grade. You could tell by the principal's intimate tone that she was just talking to Sister Jeremiah. My brother'd had her too. I was a Myles, and was inevitably compared to Terry who was considered so much better than me. Just a big show-off, really. It was much worse than a uniform, sliding into that every year. Anyway, the nun said to the other nun, Sister, the following girls have bought uniforms this year. Corcoran, Reedy, O'Donahue, Tucci, Murphy...The list trailed on. I was anxiously awaiting my name. Sister, is this list complete? Are these all the girls in 3C who have bought uniforms from the Allen Company this year? Nuns have a very precise and burdened way of speaking. Everyone is being asked to be obedient all the time. The company was probably checking up on their stinking money. I raised my hand. Yes, Eileen. They didn't call my name. Eileen Myles, Sister. The loud-speaker was two-way. It was creepy. When you travel in former communist countries you hear about the radio that even today is still on, in the walls, playing that one station. They were our enemies, the communists, but we are just like them. Could you send her down?

A little excitement. I had to go to the office. It was down the brown hall, so broad and empty. I rose. I gained the attention of the room. Eileen Myles. Everyone watching my body, I felt. In my uniform. My feet on the wooden floor, passing the blackboard, almost to the door. I stopped. Sisst...I was turning now. What is it, Eileen. The Allen Company is waiting for you. Nuns were always irritated at me. I hung my head low and then I said it. I got my uniform last year. Cause, really, I had forgot. She just looked at me like you are the stupidest little asshole that ever lived. It was angry and cringing and she was shaking her head. Sister...she kept trying to get the loud speaker's attention. It was too late. They were all down there in the office waiting for me. The company and the principal and I just didn't even know what year it was. When I got my uniform. I just knew I had it on. Everyone was laughing just like in my family. Ah-hah. That triumphant laugh. Ah-hah. Sit down, the nun screamed. John Higgins, will you bring this down to the office. She was writing a note in her perfect nun penmanship in her beautiful black and gold pen how this girl in her class didn't even know it was 1958.

For a long time we could wear any white shirt we wanted under our uniforms, but then they got over that. There were regulation Peter Pan collar shirts. Not cool ones, though. These were utterly round, like girls in story books. Very ugly shirts. And there was nothing you could do. It was different in high school, but we're not there yet.

In these uniforms I thought about breasts for the first time. Blood. And snot. One day in seventh grade I made an incredible sneeze that went flying all over my face. The nun, Sister Marisol, who taught math, thought I was laughing, so she ran over and slapped me across the face and then her hand was covered with snot. I went running out of the room, which was roaring. The boy I had a crush on that year, Chuckie Breslin, went up and took his handkerchief out of his pocket and stooped (because he was tall) and closed the door delicately. It was a riot, my friends said. The doorknob was covered with snot. Long strands of it. Splat, hitting the floor.

We called the toilet the basement. I remember crying there a lot. I never thought of myself as lonely when I was a kid, but I really was. I was always going to the bathroom because it was the only place you could be alone. It was so ugly. Big ochre-colored tiles. I mean dark, aged. The ceiling was dirty old cement. Gradually I had friends, and we would sneak in there during recess and wet wads of toilet paper and fling them really hard against the ceiling and they would make these little piles of turds. It was really great for a while. Then the voice would come. You'd do something for a while, it'd be fun and then one day the principal would come over the loud-speaker and inform us all that someone was throwing toilet paper around in the lavatory. This must cease. And it did, because the next stage was that the voice would want names and they would get names because someone would always turn you in. It was an opportunity to be good. It was not vague what good and bad were. You could really know if you didn't mind knowing the same thing as everyone else. It's what our uniforms were about. Faith. Yet boys had a wider berth for creativity in garb. I remember those knitted ties in the 50s when mothers were dressing boys. And big corduroy pants which really stunk when they peed and it seemed that boys peed a lot. Girls didn't do it so much. I wonder if this is known. Then boys got tighter pants and pointed shoes and thin ties. You would look at boys' asses. We're moving towards high school now. And surprise, I would dream about being a boy, or else about getting one and I would follow his haircut, him getting one, then growing out and looking good because there was little else to do. If the boy I liked got hit by the nun and his hair was getting long, then it would swing around and he'd get all red and it'd be really great. Then I would get hit. I would never cry. I was the only girl who ever got hit, but I'm talking about boys right now.

One boy, David Burns, was a total clown. He was always making incredible faces and doing things that would get us all in hysterics. Between each room was a door. A nun would go out, say, and leave the door open and ask the other nun to watch her room. It was like we were babies. So the nuns had struck the deal, and the other nun was heading back to her board and we were all in that crucial moment of watching a nun go away, our heads lifted towards the doorway. David, as a clown, had incredible timing, so he took that moment to get up on his chair and do something incredibly goofy. It was very Jerry Lewis. He was wagging his tongue like a dog, and he was humping and wiggling his hips, it was just a little gross moment of comedy. Really hysterical. Because the nun behind him had turned around at the last moment, and right behind him salivating and dancing was her looking at him and us in horror. In some ways it was the funniest moment in my life. The silent horror of him getting caught doing the dog. It was parents coming down, the whole thing. It was necessary. It had to be, but it was so lovely.

Sister Jamesetta's name meant Little James, and she always informed the children of this on the first day of school. You got it right up front: her weird vanity about being small and her silly name and her one tiny joke. She was the potato chip nun. They all had little jobs like that, distributing, selling, and controlling something. So a big box of potato chips was delivered to this small nun at the beginning of each month. She would open them, and that would be a big deal. Got a boy to help. The loud rip. Then it was always open, the big brown box, and it was in the aisle next to the window, and on this particular day she was teaching math and she was backing up. She fell in. Her little nun shoes, small heels, tapered toes with tiny holes. Her black stockings. The little legs kicking. Her skirts raised about to lower calf. Would somebody please help me, she screamed. Her butt all over the potato chips. Charles, somebody. Class, stop laughing. It was just unbelievable. We had never seen a nun trapped before. So well-lit by the window with daylight flooding in. Sister Jamesetta. And no one would buy those chips. It was a silent strike, a joke. There is nothing wrong with these potato chips, she would insist, when day after day at the pre-lunch potato chip moment when we were all totally ravenous no one would go up, get in line for the weird communion. She farted on them. That was the word. They're perfectly good. They're gross. Which we got to say by default.

We were walking up stairs for years and there was a broken statue on the third landing and I did it. I crashed into it or something. After many years of thinking that was probably the worst thing in the world you could do. When you get up there to the eighth grade, just think if you smash into that white and colored statue which celebrated the Immaculate Conception, which just meant Mary, appearing to kids somewhere. Mary was always there for a conversation. She was white and there were lambs.

December 8th was Mary's feast. I was born on the 9th, the day after. I bumped into her statue and chipped it and then I had to live with that for a couple of years. It made me feel sick every time we took the landing, which was several times a day. Always God, the whole story hanging over our world like a parrot. We were always having to commemorate, to color things in. Holy things.

You'd be doing math, a piece of old newsprint with blue equations, and when you finished you could color in Mary. I shot through my math…this is maybe second grade and I had a very large box of Crayola, perfect for the job and I colored her robes in white which was correct and then I did each tiny bead on her outfit in gold. It looked really good, in fact I was embarrassed. Good on good. So I wrote in little tiny letters at the top of the paper, "Pretty good, huh, teach." I was pretending to be a public school kid. I passed it in and then I felt really sick. Next day the paper came back with a demand that I show it to my mother. You did such a beautiful job with your coloring and then you write something like this. And not even Sister. Show this to your family. Sure. What I did was scribble over my comments. Leaving hers and a big patch of scribbling. Then I showed my mother and told her that when a girl in front of me saw how pretty I colored Mary she scribbled on my paper. But I didn't want to turn her in. So I got in trouble. My mother seemed a little confused, but she could see that I was good. She wasn't paying attention at all. She signed it dutifully. It was like everyone, nuns, parents, was a routing clerk, checking our little lives off as we sailed by on something, a huge cloud that was bigger than everyone. I brought the paper into class and told the nun that my mother was disgusted by what I wrote and that's why she scribbled on it. The nun seemed to have forgotten what I was talking about. She was going through menopause, there were seventy kids in the class that year and I was just one of them. I figured I was magic.

I hate to even talk about the high school part but I will. The uniforms were wool, red and grey. Those mother-fuckers call today, the alumni association, same little twinks, and they ask me on the phone, what do you do. I am a lesbian poet I say. You're a poet, says some girl named Valerie or Sheila, Catholic names. Would you like to tell us something about your work life. Yes. I have just published a book. Oh, thank you, says the girl. I would like to give you its title and the name of the publisher. Oh that won't be necessary. May I tell you about the reunion.

Assholes.

There were little metal buttons, four silver ones on our double-breasted vests. Weskits, the nuns called them. Your weskit. It was deeply similar to the waitressing outfits worn in a chain called the Pewter Pot that reigned in Boston in the 60s. It was sort of a Renaissance tart look. We were being prepared to be waitresses or what? Wives. Ladies. The only thing you need to know about high school is that my brother was the president of the junior class which was typical. He was always this big finky boss. We were friends, though, at this point. Terry and I drank together, watched Johnny Carson, and I advised him on his clothes.

Then along came Ascension Thursday. A holy day of obligation, which meant no school and a beach party was planned. We went to Crane's, which was everyone's favorite beach. It was private. Really big dunes, perfect for drinking. My brother's friend Andy could buy. We were into Colt 45. Have yourself a truly unique experience. So in the cafeteria everyone gave Terry money. He drove up to Crane's in my mother's white Falcon. Put all that Colt in the trunk. I think Terry got really smashed. I was up to my regular stuff—crawling around the dunes with Gary. He was kind of a big baby, but I always had this compulsion to imitate him. I liked his walk. I think I identified tremendously with Gary, but since I was a girl and he was a boy we were required to go off and have sex.

But I didn't want to stroke his dick which was what he wanted. We'd get drunk and I would submit to his rough awkward kisses. He was an articulate kid, a poet, but in these moments it was like he was Dutch. Terry came home drunk that day, I'm sure, but none of this is what you need to know.

I went to the Arlington Catholic reunion this year, and everyone kept asking, How's Terry? Carol Driscoll who emceed the event wouldn't let up. Once she got good and tanked she asked trivia questions. Here's one for you, Eileen Myles. Who...got expelled for drinking beer at Crane's Beach on Ascension Thursday? Was that 1965? Did your brother get expelled or suspended. Her drunken voice kept changing pitch. Can you straighten me out on this, she asked.

The voice began talking about Arlington Catholic students getting drunk on Ascension Thursday. It started like that on the next day in school. Then the forms came down. More newsprint with faded blue text. It was a questionnaire. Did you go to Crane's Beach on Ascension Thursday. Who did you ride with. Was there liquor in the car. Did you drink at Crane's Beach. How much. Where did you get this liquor. Did you see other people drinking? Who were they? How would you describe their behavior?

I just remember a sea of no's on my form. Terry wasn't in school that day. I think he was sick. He had ulcers so he always got away with a lot around health. Have your students filled in their forms? Will you send them down, Sister. Then names began to be called. I don't think I was called down. It was mainly boys. And Susie Martel. She was always a big boozer. We all thought it was the senior girls who turned everyone in. They had really tight little permanents and bad skin and were all very holy and going to Regis. National Merit Scholars. But looking back it could be Mark Shack. They called down all the boys on the football team. Who were all there and drinking. The big families. It was those families, the ones that were very special to the parish. Because of their contributions to the church or sports. That's what mattered. Good Catholic families playing sports. Getting ready to go to good Catholic colleges. Once in a while being Catholic at Harvard or Tufts. Hardly ever Harvard. Being Catholic at Villanova. BC. My brother *was* expelled. Nobody else. My mother went down to the rectory to talk to Monsignor Oscar O'Gorman, a horrible old man that everyone hated but he built our parish into something rich. He wouldn't even speak to my mother. The decision is made, Madam, he said. Because we weren't rich, my mother said. Because my father was dead. She was alone. My brother was punished for these things.

I had a choice. I never wanted to go to Catholic school. I wanted to go to Arlington High with my greaser friends. My mother forced me to go to Arlington Catholic. And I could leave now if I wanted. Terry was leaving. I remember standing out in the yellow hallways of the first floor totally sobbing, I didn't know why. It just seemed fucked- up that my brother had been thrown out. The nun who taught me Latin passed by and said, you look like you lost your best friend. She was being sarcastic. Yes I did, and I kept crying.

# 24.

Over my head were fireworks going off. Big sprays of them, peach, green and white over the mid-summer sky. Was Fourth of July the middle of summer. Beginning, the end? I could never figure it out. Tonight I was on crutches. It was 1981. On the corner of 2nd Street and First Avenue in the yellow light of the liquor store. The sidewalk had that tan color dirty cement gets in neon light. Oddly warm and sickening. Just like an acid trip. Splatters of old black gum. Flip tops. Stubbed out cigarettes. Just a New York sidewalk in all its pebbly, bumpy, cordoned-off beauty. It was warm. It was fucking hot. I was over-dressed in jeans and a teeshirt. Just standing there. On crutches. They were digging into my armpits and I was so tired.

I needed to cry but I couldn't. It was like the fireworks were crying for me. I couldn't move. I was stuck on that corner with my pile of change in my pocket, just enough, about three twenty nine, for a bottle of red wine. Sour. No one was coming over that I knew of. It was just for me. It was about a half hour before the liquor store closed. I just had to get there and I would, but right now I had to hold still for a moment and suffer quietly. Because this was a terrible life, a sorrowful life, which I felt I had not been prepared for in any way.

I mourned the buildings and the sky and my warm change and my dirty hands, the fact that I needed a bath and a drink. I needed a drink. I needed a drink like mosquitoes needed blood. Sweat needs to get out.

A phone has to ring. I had to get to that light. Inside was a man behind a wall of thick plastic. I'd like one of those. He nodded. Slid it to me in a brown paper bag. Then I walked. I was clutching that bottle tight. I wouldn't drop it. The pads of the crutches jabbed into my pits but I was swinging home. I always count. 62, 63, 64, 65...

# In the West

# 1.

There was a time in my life when I was just taste. It held me there, strong. I think it was a baby place, and I couldn't get it out of my mind that if I could taste the right thing, and keep it in mind, I would know where to begin. The day was some rungs that I knew with my mouth. San Francisco was how I left that state, I was looking for something more open, another. I got caught. I didn't know the next. I was leaving home. In the middle of that I was a baby. The puffy sleeves and the puffy face. A small stranger riding on a train next to some other 70s-looking person. I remember a big box, a cardboard box in the middle of the room in the house that I left in Cambridge. Everything was in there. Just pieces of paper, junk, skis. Would you like these, Anne?

How many times do you leave your room. When my family had picnics we would use this yellow basket. I put a blanket in it and a can of cat food, actually two, and a buck. I popped my cat in, one I didn't really care about. I put the basket on the steps of a doctor's office a few doors up on Magazine Street. The cat simply pushed against the lid with her head and walked out, turning once to give me a look. It didn't bode well for my trip. I handed the gerbil cage to the kids next door. If their mother objected, I didn't speak Spanish. It was a grey street, not one I'd miss, heading down to the obvious of obvious, Charles River. It exists to have hotels on its bank. Goodbye Charles!

I spent a night in Montreal, lying on my bed looking at the lights across the street. It was the cheesiest feeling in the world, the neon pink, the bright green. I had foldable shutters on my window, I preferred to keep them open, open to the world. Honking, and razzing me. Being alive. I will. The breeze on my nostrils. And then I fell asleep.

The blueness of Vancouver. I should stay here I thought, while I was there, but I couldn't. The perfection of air and mountains and big hotels. One French Canadian laughing at the queen. We sat drinking hard cider in a bar in Gastown. Indians came in to sell their wares and I was impressed. Jesus, this is old. The skinny building at the corner, with an "o" for a clock. Lookit this. This is the West, this is the past. It's not the East Coast. My sister came. We were like runaways. Her big floppy hats, wanting to be Maria Schneider. I walked her through that. Wondering if I could get a tattoo. Should I be journalist. Or a whore. She left, thank God. Wanting to be Mary Tyler Moore. I was masculine, a bit. Walking down hills.

One place, a guy ran out and said, do you want to be in a commercial. We'll give you some drinks. I said sure. I had some tequila sunrises, sitting on a pillow. Velvet ones thrown around. We were all lounging, *now dance*. We got up. I remember a man down on his knees, shooting up at me. Cool, I thought. I love San Francisco. Do you want to do some cocaine, these guys asked. Around thirty it seemed to me. Tanned, probably gay though I didn't think that exactly. You want to go to Finocchio's, watch drag. Okay, yeah. No, I just want a Coke. Are you sure. Are you sure? Beer, yeah, okay a beer. You don't smoke. Yeah, well okay. Not always. I like your shirt. Thank you.

My shirt had shirts on it. Lots of little shirts. It was tight. My shoes were about three colors. I met these girls, they were all secretaries. They all lived in one apartment on Twin Peaks. They sort of took me in for a while. Watching teevee on their big beige rug. I didn't get it, though. You just came here to be secretaries? I can't believe you can do that. I have such a burden. I don't know, but something. I think a writer. I lived in all these teeny little rooms, then I moved. It was up on a hill. It seemed clean there. Because it was a different style, I couldn't tell if it was rich or not. Seemed kind of rich. I think it costs money to live high. I had this window. Little rectangle looking out on the bay. One hundred and twenty dollars a month. I had a little air plant that lived in a glass. Was that enough. No water? Nobody seemed to know. Why did you get an air plant. That's sort of sad.

I met men everywhere I went. I was going insane. I don't know where I met the man who wound up singing to me. Amadeo, something like that. He gave me some wine. He picked up his guitar and he started to sing. I thought I was completely going to lose it right there. I've got to go. There was this guy who brought me to a party with his friends. Out on Sunset. He had a convertible. You think it'd be nice, but it wasn't. All that air blowing in my face. I really hate air. Sailboats, all that. What's the pleasure, I don't get it. Anyway it was just like all these people from Arlington except they were from California. Having a cookout. He was a nice man. I mean you could see that he was trying to figure something out as well as being attracted to me. Was I attractive? I was just being female. That's all I felt. Somedays fat, somedays thin.

What did you eat. I can't remember eating. I remember trying to not eat. I met this guy named Peter at Vesuvio's. He was cute. His eyes were kind of closed, He just didn't look so American. While fucking me he said, "I never balled a plump chick before." I think that was the first mean thing anyone ever said to me. Where I thought, that's mean. Amazing. I mean, how did he say that? Me, a plump chick. I think he was a writer too. I kept starting this novel that began with the gerbils running around in their cage. "Gerbils are running around in their cage. This is my life. I am 22." Shit. The paper I used was that wrinkly oniony kind and sometimes it even had red lines. The typewriter was heavy and blurry so it just didn't look good. I don't think I ever wrote a poem. One about the air plant of course.

You ran away from home. That's what he said. Could I tell him Mrs. Currin my Irish literature professor said that Joyce said that the artist must renounce family, home, country, religion, all of it. So I had to get rid of everything. That's what I was doing here. But then there was nothing to hold onto. I am 22. The night the Sunset man, maybe his name was Phil, took me home I began to hear all those voices. I would lie down on my head, as if I could sleep and I could never sleep. The cacophony would begin. Jabber-jabber-jabber-jabber-jabber. Millions and millions of voices. Absolutely everyone and no one. The thing I knew was that I had to keep hearing all of them. Keeping everyone at equal weight. Because if not, then one voice would come forward, that really weird one, kind of taunting and high-pitched, it seemed homosexual to me. It was alluring and it would completely take control and I would never come back. So I had to keep them all important and I couldn't sleep. Dawn. Still awake, motor running inside. Fear. Walk out into the kitchen, pick up the glass with the airplant in it. What is that?

I had many jobs of course. When I was wandering around with my sister we discovered this gourmet cafeteria across from the Currin Theater. All the men who worked there were blond. It was strange because being hired made me sort of suspect I was young enough and good-looking enough. There was no other way to tell, having no middle or home. Here you got quiche, soup. San Joaquin valley vegetable soup. Just a pronunciation like San Joaquin would keep me alive for a few days. People always talked about sex. Not everyone was gay, but lots of people. There was a woman named Kitty who I loved. I loved her ass. It was a beautiful small rounded ass, and as I was not a lesbian, it was disturbing, this love. It raised the attention given to a thing to a level like religion or something. Again and again I would turn to it. Think of it. Her tight little ass in her tight little pants. Finally every time I saw it was like the million sounds in my head. There was no *once*. In Boston when the Berrigans were arrested and so was Sister Mary McAllister, I felt that way about her. A woman's face, a cute face, a nun's. It was on the cover of the Boston Globe, this young political woman, and I loved her. And a paper does happen again and again. One day walking around loving this woman. Her black and white face. Her soft brown bangs. I was printing her. I was a huge factory inventing this woman again and again. She was so beautiful. Kitty's ass hung by the coffee station in red jeans. She chose to confide in me. Eric doesn't have too much going on up here, she tapped her head, but he's a good fuck. But he knows it. She gave me new language. Someone could be a good fuck. She had bangs, medium-brown hair. Kind of short, kind of long, a bob I guess you'd say. Eric wasn't gay, that's what was good about him. I think she said that too. I'm sure she felt me staring at her. How could she not. You kind of lose waitressing jobs in this cool way. The job withdraws. There was another blond guy who wore baseball caps and he was straight too. He asked me to a baseball game. I hated sports, I had hated them all my life but people always assumed I liked them. I'd go, just sit there like a camel, wanting more beers, never having enough. At one point the field would flash all green and I'd be happy for a moment. It wasn't the air I hated, it was all the people. Millions of them and their focus. Down there. This guy was as shaky as I was. He said he was at a point where he was going to have to become either a Jesus freak or a fag. I looked at him. Did it have to be like that. This was California. There were bodies turning up in graves every day. It seemed so normal to find dead boys' bodies on the news. It was like people liked it. It would be so easy to kill me. Anyone could. That's why I didn't like it. It was just a small coincidence, my life. One of those sad girls. Even back in Boston, someone took me to a Robert Bresson film in which a girl throws herself out a window. You remind me of her, he said. Hope you don't think that's too weird. Oh no, I said. She was beautiful. With her blonde grey hair. A funny tone that looked nice on film.

Anyway, it was Candlestick Park we were sitting in. It seemed like he was going to choose Christian. At least he didn't want to fuck me. He was weak. People who think there are two choices are even worse off than me. I resist millions. Horrible day after horrible day. I met this man who owned a bar on Broadway. I think his name was Leon. He was a fat old bald man, but kind of a hipster. I suppose I met him in another bar. It was in strip joint territory. He took me to some bathhouse. It was all pale green sweating walls. Brick. I was expected to take my clothes off and I did. I let him touch my body, rub some oils on it. I think I feel like Jesus I thought. Just being dead, that's all. I guess I was supposed to fuck him, suck him off in there. In all that grease. No, I said softly. I was not a good little whore. I would just sort of slide. An old man would just want some access to my body. Just to be around my youth. I felt that. I went back to his apartment. He had those curtains that had all sorts of people fucking on them. Erotic. That's why the word still creeps me out. I think of old people's curtains. He bought me a cup. We went to a crafts fair and there was this ceramic chalice. It was blue and tan, kind of pretty. I swear it cost fifty dollars. You want that, he asked. Yeah, I said looking at him. Forked it right over. Leon. At whatever moment in my life I decided he must have died I still had that chalice. Leon. I gave it a kiss.

There was a man with a ponytail who sat in Vesuvio's and drank beers. He asked me to dinner. We went to the Jones Diner in Chinatown. He said this was the best place. It was okay. I enjoyed being fed. He was old again. He had been married, but it broke up. They had some kids. Close to your age, I bet. He looked at me. He smoked a lot, he seemed sad and lonely. I was basically against divorce. Someone would be happy to have this man.

In waitressing they take away one shift and then they take away another and then you feel paranoid and start dropping things. They either actually fire you or they take away your last shift so there's no time for you to come in. You might eat once and leave an apron and that's that. Or they may bother to fire you. It's lousy work. I hated it. Serving people food is the worst. All that delight you have to stomach. And I always get deranged on one substance or another. Something I just can't stop eating. The tall man who hired me is probably dead. Kitty's 47 or 48.

I went to sit in the park one day. Washington Square Park. The one in San Francisco. With the big church there. And the hill. I was thinking Amadeo's apartment is over there. I hope he doesn't come around. I was just sitting on the grass and I hadn't gotten much sleep and I was thinking the same big questions I always thought about: where should I go, what should I do, and slowly I seeped into this other thing. I was not connected. Something was sitting there but it was not " I." No I, not at all. I saw church, green grass, no I. I was not connected. Didn't know what grass was, didn't know what words were. The thing that had so delicately connected these things was gone and I was suspended in not being, not knowing, not having a body, not experiencing myself, no trivial thought, no complaint. Surrounded but not attached. Not closer or further from the surface, but simply not "in" at all. Not outside either. It wasn't like a movie. Losing, simply losing. I got up. In the middle of that. There was a hill. I took it. No, that didn't bring me closer. I saw an ice cream shop. Chocolate. I bit into it. Nothing. No mouth. No there. Chocolate, yes, but so what. Kept walking. Opened apartment door. Got in shower. Hot, cold. Hot, cold. Slowly something came back and I returned. I had been empty of me. I didn't want that.

There was a little job I had down in the financial district. Bank of America. Filing student loans. A huge wall of folders, a large sweeping wing of a mechanism. They moved up, they moved down. I was there all day. Behind me a huge window and all the buildings were out there. It was blue as heaven. Dark blue. It was day. It was better to work, that was for sure. Look at that. The Bank of California. Wells Fargo. How really West.

After work I found a little bar that reminded me of Boston's stockbroker scene. An old little bar tucked away. I got used to going there after work and stuffing my face with pretzels and chicken wings. Some guy would offer me a drink. Sure gin and tonic. He'd usually lose interest fast, I was so boring. I'd just stand there and smoke. How did I ever survive. I closed the place one night with a guy. I was really bombed. I wanted to go a little farther with somebody. He had short hairs combed onto his forehead a little bit. He was a businessman, a salesman. Really creepy, in the beginning, but I got used to him. Writer, huh. Astronaut, marine biologist, what the fuck. I'll buy you some more, he said. I was shaking my pack. What do you smoke, Parliaments. I nodded. He threw them down on the table. He smoked Newports. I've got a great idea, Arlene. Since we're both kind of new around here, why don't we go to Fisherman's Wharf and get some seafood. Whaddya say. He lifted his glass and threw back the ice, but his little eye was looking at me like one of those whales that surface for a moment. I'm kind of broke, I said. My treat, Arlene. I'm really enjoying talking to you here. I shrugged and we were off.

I think it's a sin. It was a sin when Leon touched my body. I just thought you're lying here and you're lying. You just can't get up. I'd like to pick up the cup he brought me, to lift it again. We sat down at a table in this huge restaurant. It was black outside. We were near water. I'm a girl. He would light my cigarette. I couldn't read the menu. My head was swimming. I got another drink. I was obedient to the situation. I tasted it. It was like everything was liquid, everywhere. We got these big bowls of soup, red in tureens with thousands of fish with legs in them. Shrimps, everything bobbing. It was probably delicious but it seemed awful. My drinks kept lining up around me. Don't you have any money, he asked at some ridiculous time. He was presenting me with a bill. His face was wide. His hair was short. I think his name was Martin. Marty. I think we even got a drink at the end, one of those double shot things like a rusty nail. Amazing. He carried me out. The bed was spinning in his motel. Take your dress off, he said. I'm comfortable, I said. Do you want to take a shower, he asked. I just wanted to lie in the dark. He took his shirt off. His pants. He had socks on still and BVDs. He had little skinny legs and one of those old men wide flat bodies with a little belly. It was just like if he lied down flat he'd be big pancake. His nakedness was really creepy. Just seeing his body made me feel stronger. But somehow I got my dress off. I feel like a man. Just to be even remembering this. Then he pulled his underpants off. A little dick. He kept putting spit on it and whacking it. It was like it didn't matter what I saw. It was weird. C'mon help me, he said. So I helped him. He didn't want to kiss me. He didn't want to hold me. His little dick wouldn't get hard. Get down there, he said. Just kiss it, he asked. It was like his spit I couldn't stop thinking of. The dick, that little thing was nothing. It was dark. I mean it was pretty dark, just from outside. I remember sucking on his stupid little dick. Rub your tits against my legs. C'mon. I had really small breasts. I tried.

It was like touching someone. Shake your tits. Pull yourself up a little bit, so I can see them. I couldn't do it. C'mon shake your tits. It felt stupid. I couldn't do it. Why was the salesman demanding a show. Why did I have to do it. Shake them, shake them, please. He was jerking himself off by now. C'mon. C'mon. C'mon. It was so dark in his motel room. Shake your tits, shake your tits. The cars going by made scars on the walls. It was dark. C'mon shake. I shook.

# To Go Home

# 1.

I might be making this up, but the house I grew up in only cost my parents $13,000. It seems so cheap for a house, even a house in Arlington, even a house right off Arlington Center, at the end of a dead end street. Even a house with a sub shop on the corner, and a dry cleaners opposite that. My house you had to cross the train tracks to get to. To watch the Boston & Maine railroad clank by in the morning and those men reading papers going to work. It was so sad to learn that those men weren't coming from Maine, but Lexington, the next town over. But I didn't learn that for years, not until I was in college at the University of Massachusetts where I learned facts like that. In a state university you learn about your roots, what you've been seeing all your life.

I was afraid of our house. Not like my brother who saw it once from Lombard Street, which was essentially the back, and there it was, bright as a moon, my house from the other side. It made Terry sick, it made me happy, that there was an "out." Somewhere I could stand and look at our house. My brother resisted this point of view; I thought it was hope. Our house was so cheap because of what happened in it. To the two girls who once lived in the room, my sister and mine. It's amazing to think that we knew.

Mrs. Lobrino lived downstairs. It was a two family house, and we bought it and she was already there, a link to the past. We bought it and she didn't leave her home. We left her there. I don't think she died. She was there for a little while. She had see-through curtains different from ours on her door. She was an older woman, probably a widow and she became my mother's friend because my mother instantly became a daughter to women of the right age, she would be their younger friend. And they would give her things and show her things. Next door were the Aulenbachs and Mr. Aulenbach who was quite bald gave my mother the first red rose of the season. I seem to remember it that way, and I don't know how his wife felt, who was well and alive. They had a white trellis crawling with roses and this man would give a red rose to my mother and it would be part of her joy, of her sweetness. She was such a daughter, my mom. She was so perfect. Mrs. Lobrino gave us sauce.

I remember the foreign bowl of it, the deep orange red with big sausages bobbing, a meatball or two. She'd make too much and at some point she'd ship some up to us. The phone would ring. A black phone, all rounded and harsh, heavy and adult. My mother would pick it up. *Terryeileebridgie*...would you go downstairs. I'd come up carrying it. It'd be a tureen, a really big bowl, pink Italian looking, with this tremendous foreign food dark orange bobbing. I can't remember the woman's face. I remember the bowl, her handing it to me.

Behind our house, on the side that eventually led to Lombard Street, there was a yard. There was a big fence right below our second floor door, our back door, and there was those people's yard and their immense garden. And you know my mother was dropping it, putting down a pan on a rope, and the people down there who she simply smiled at their garden said, Genny would you like some Swiss chard. She would. I remember that stuff. My mother liked to grow things and she was a fan of people who had roses and vegetables and liked to cook, they were old these people, and they missed their families, and my mother had one and we were endlessly receiving shipments of food from these people.

I want you to get the hang of the house, where I lived from three to twenty-one, eighteen years. Sort of internment, sort of beautiful. The house had an immense chestnut tree in its yard and beyond that, many houses and then the miracle of Spy Pond with, in its exact center, an island. Revolutionary spies hid there, we had been told. Everyone's worlds are flooded with stories. Legends of the past. My town was so old and cool. A little wooden house sat there on the edge of the pond. You could see the pond frozen, my mother could watch us, skating. The characteristic of Arlington I know the most is our visibility. My place in her eye. Moving through my town, the overall sensation of mother, watching. At some point they knocked down the wooden house which I failed to mention was the Arlington Boys Club. A source of distress for me. Where's the Girls Club, I screamed. They flung up a larger structure, much larger and it was blue. They wrote the words in white type on its outside. Not just above the door. Arlington Boys Club. It blocked my mother's view of the pond and I could never look at that blue building without wincing at the crime, the erasure of girls. My mother felt bad because she couldn't see the pond. Though we weren't skating anymore.

What's important is the sauce. The hands of the woman downstairs, her old seventy-year-old hands extending this meal to us. There may have been pasta too. There was. I don't think she died in our house.

I asked my mother once. I was sitting at her table. Did you learn to make this sauce from Rosie? She was my aunt's upstairs neighbor, in Somerville. Their house was a three-decker which they didn't own, rented for years. Rosie was the landlady, the wife of the owner, Frankie. Their name was Marcone. I thought of sound. The smell of the hallway was theirs, the incredible odor of red tomato sauce, cheese and oil, the delicious stink of Italian food, my favorite, wafting, inhabiting, coming down. There were newspapers, there was linoleum, baseball and yells. But mostly there were smells. My aunt's sauce was derived from the methods of Rosie. And yours, Mom. Mrs. Lobrino. Of course, of course. She was proud of her independence. Her learning from Lobrino. And Lobrino saved the girls.

The people who owned the house before us were this woman and this man. The man was not the girls' father and the woman worked nights and he would, you know, do things to the girls. They weren't supposed to tell, he told them that, some kind of threat and they didn't for a long time, they were like our age. Me and Bridgie's. I just remember being eleven or twelve, and someone telling us about this. But eventually the girls told Mrs. Lobrino, who was probably handing them some sauce, which is better than a gun, which is like safety. They told her while she was giving them food, and she went inside and picked up the heavy black phone, I bet Mrs. Lobrino had the heaviest, and you didn't even dial, you just said give me the police, she did that and they came and the man went to jail. The girls were free. So I knew two things. This had happened in my room where I lived with my sister, we knew evil things had happened in the dark there and we could always feel it, we always could, and that sauce was good.

I opened the mailbox and out it came. It was a yellow manila envelope with a red and blue label that said Westborough State Hospital on the outside. I didn't tell anyone. I didn't tell my mother or my brother. I haven't told the lawyer. It says there was no money when Nellie died. She died intestate. It means broke.

$13,000 isn't much for a house. My cousin Brian was outside running around. He wore Indian moccasins with tanned legs and he kicked up gravel in the thin driveway between the three houses on the base of the L that ended my street. My cousin's feet were spraying tiny rocks. He must have been twelve. The picture of my grandmother is a bad xerox. It's on the top of the pile. There's hands around Nellie's neck, so her head won't fall down. Her hair's pulled back. It looks black. I guess I could go demand the original. Each sheet from my grandmother's records, there's about ten, has the hands of the man who xeroxed them. He's wearing a ring and his shirt is striped. Nellie's old records were awkward so the man had to lean and press to get it all. He was a state employee, a law student, I bet.

I'm grateful to the state of Massachusetts. For letting me live in a house, with a view of an island, for educating me, at least for one year in public schools and then for four years—for giving me a high quality low tuition public education. I would not be a writer if not for the University of Massachusetts (Boston). I think this is the place to thank the state.

My Nellie Riordan, my grandmother Nellie, was born in Ireland in 1880. The state gives me facts. Her story is the saddest in the world. Sadder than my house. Nellie was born in Ireland, a beautiful place. Her father was a farmer. A man named John. He lived to "about" 90, Massachusetts thinks. John Riordan's wife was Mary, Mary Cooper. She lived to about 80. In 1940 there was an interview.

Massachusetts, on the occasion of my grandmother's admission into the state mental hospital, sat down with my father ("lives at home, unemployed"), my uncle (Ed, the white haired one) and Nellie's husband, Terrance, and together they erected some facts. Which lay there on paper for forty years. The story was very simple. She wasn't feeling well. It was 1940.

She came to America in 1900. To a Boston port, it said. In 1908 she got married in Charlestown to my grandfather, Terrance Myles. She was naturalized through him. He was 21, she was 28. It's not fiction. The records are very clear on that. They say her husband was seven years her junior. Repeatedly. It's an important fact, low-value wife, a worker and a breeder. She was cleaning houses all those years. Between immigration and marriage. And, of course, during. I don't think my grandmother was pretty. I think it's a Kennedy thing, the men are better looking than the women. That's how it is in some families. She had very dark hair. My mother says. She's the girl on the cliff, I know. And Nellie started popping them out, her kids. We don't need names. It's 1940. She wasn't feeling well. She was sixty. The records say Nellie was always "inclined somewhat to look on the dark side of things." She came here in 1900, famine. Maybe not so good. Half the population of Ireland died of starvation that year. And the Irish were denounced from the Anglican pulpits while they were starving them. Lazy. The Irish brought this upon themselves, the Irish Catholics. You don't always hear about the true conditions of the "Irish Potato Famine," how the pigs and the grain and the eggs went to England while the potato remained, but when it went bad, the Irish were to blame. The landlords made their tenants tear down their own houses if they couldn't pay the rent. My grandmother left. We don't hear much about this, that they were starved out of their country, because the Irish were ashamed. They just came here and forgot what it was like to see your family die of hunger. I guess I just want to say that Nellie probably came here and cleaned the houses of the relatives of the same people who drove her out of her home, who took all the food except the potatoes, which were rotting that year. Teeth lost: 32.

She had none, when she got to Westborough. Having kids depletes vitamins, you can certainly lose your teeth that way. And it's probably hereditary as well. It's a joke how bad the teeth are in Dublin, beautiful city, but Jesus, get a dentist. There's simply no way to find out whose houses my grandmother cleaned. It's a fact to forget. Like Ireland.

She was not feeling well so she went to the doctor. He said, you have high blood pressure and hardening of the arteries. Nellie hit the roof. She started worrying. She couldn't sleep. She stopped cleaning the house. She had always been a very good housekeeper, the records said. My grandmother was a professional. Her sole interest was centered in her family. I'm done, I'm done, she cried. And who would take care of them. She was wringing her hands. Her husband and the brothers and the one daughter Helen would be leaving the house in the morning and she said I'll be dead when you get back. You'll never see me again. Nellie sounded furious. Why didn't somebody stay home. Better to spend your life tied to a chair at home than in the arms of Massachusetts. She walked around and around. Lost interest in everything. Stayed in bed a great deal of the time. Then Helen died. It had been a routine operation. Appendicitis. It just went bad. At first the brothers and her husband thought the shock of it, losing her 27-year-old girl, seemed to snap her out of it, "the nervous breakdown." For a few days it did. She started cooking dinner again, cleaning the house and things seemed good. She was her usual cheery self, they told Massachusetts. Then she got worse.

I am sitting with my family, I'm eight or nine—ten, and suddenly a rocket takes off on television and at that instant I became a space traveller, an astronaut. I began to know the joy of being alone in space. Away from my family in their tiny little house with so much trouble and pain. The beauty of it, the glittering eternal songs. The planets bobbing. My poor parents mourning their mums and dads. And us missing them. Sad little teevee, black and white and my family sitting cozy, close together one night. I took off in my ship to see the night and the lights of the world. I'm the first girl who does it. Not just the moon, but Mars and farther and farther.

In grade school we were cautioned if we couldn't draw faces we could just leave them orange. Sometimes I am flying by so fast and the people are faceless like dying stars and I am so alone. Massachusetts tells me that for two hours before she died my grandmother had visual and auditory hallucinations. I am circling her house. One morning, what day of the week, my Nellie Riordan, was flying way out and I was in school.

I stood outside Westborough one day (1995) and the color had returned. In the fifties the building was yellow, I was a small thing crawling around, waiting for those warm shaky steps. Teddy holding her by her arm. She's grinning and smiling. Her hair was straight, with a barrette. Photos took the color away. For years I looked at my family, made out of shadows, their moment rippling in light. Sensitive greys. Here's the family record, then there's the records of the state. It was so monstrous and vulgar, the mythical building, blooming here in all its yellow. The outside of her house.

I want to go home, says Nellie. She tells the nurse she is dead and that the undertaker came this morning. Franny Brown. Her children are being tortured. It is difficult to break through this stream of talk, said Massachusetts. Patient does not answer when asked where she lives. When asked if she lives in Somerville, she says, "Yes Somerville." Asked where in Somerville said, "Somewhere around Union Square." Asked what street her house is on patient said, "I don't know where is it." Asked how long she had been here patient said, "I've been here a long time." Asked if it was more than a week, she said, "I think so." Asked if it were more than a month said, "I've been here a long time." Asked if it was more than a year she said, "I don't know, it's a long time." She said spontaneously to the examiner, "You stay here with me, don't leave me alone." Massachusetts asked her if she liked this institution, She said, "This place is alright if you have to stay here." At the time of this interview (Dec. 5, 1940) patient says repeatedly, "I want to go home, I want to go home."

None of the sons reached fifty. Edward died of heart failure, Vinnie, 42, died in his sleep. John died of cirrhosis in a V.A. hospital in Mattapan. How's Frank, asked the brothers when they saw each other. Well Frank was the oldest and he stopped drinking early. Frank had a heart condition. At Ed's wake he entertained us kids with a story about feeding his cat raw kidneys. Too hard to cut, said Frank, so he and Avis let their kitty drag the purple mess across the rug all day, chewing as she liked. We laughed so hard. Uncle Frank. And the planets pulled away.

I watched my father, Terrence, die on the couch. He was changing colors and his breath became nasal, pure snot, like one gleaming part of him was left, banging in an ash can. I was stuck, couldn't get up. My mother was outside hanging clothes, the breeze was perfect that October afternoon in 1961, a great day to sail, clip some laundry on a line to dreamy softness while he was inside dying under the scrutiny of his eleven-year-old daughter's eyes who was quietly writing a punish task while his frantic butterfly squawked. *I will not talk, I will not talk*, the daughter wrote.

I suppose people are vanishing all of the time from the world. People popping out of houses, smoke escaping out of chimneys at night, a door flings open and they take them away, water drains into some bigger body, toilets flushing, the loneliness of everything moving along. The world spinning through space in the eye of the sun. God gave us the state of Massachusetts.

It continues:

General Appearance: A fairly well-developed, fairly well-nourished white woman 60 years of age. Later, a poorly-developed elderly woman. A middle aged woman. A well-nourished, well-developed...this senile woman. Thin senile woman with flabby dry very pale skin. Sometimes she died at 74, 76. The years change. Sometimes it's 1957. It's '56, it's '54. She's been at Westborough fourteen years, maybe sixteen. Sometimes it's Westboro. There's a certificate of insanity and a certificate of death. She's fidgety, the State says. At times she gestures and counts on her fingers. If she's in the ward, she prefers to be out in the hall and vice versa. Has refused food most of the time since her admission, patient often requires tube feeding.

*The Pilgrim State*

I saw it in a movie. The person is strapped down, a skinny one who wants to die. A fat man opens the skinny one's mouth and jams it in, the white tube. I have sinned, she said. According to Massachusetts, Nellie believed that she had done something in her life that was wrong and she could never be forgiven for it. I did not do that did I. I did not do that did I. They did not use commas. It's black and white, her record. Xeroxed, typewritten forms, a Nellie count, that tradition. It's Massachusetts, the solemn state, a commonwealth, that holds the Anglicans and their servants, regulates the port unto which the servants arrive. The port is a huge open mouth. America, this country of food, from sea to sea, and the State lets down his plastic nipple, a tube, and he feeds Nellie. The State expresses a dense white nutritious sauce he has made for the poor. ECONOMIC CONDITION: Marginal. We are home.

In an interview on July 16, 1940, the State asked my grandmother the name of this place. Massachusetts was testing her. A: Looks like Somerville. Her voice is low-pitched, barely audible. Then my grandmother has a question for which they give her no answer. "Why are the people here being severely punished—upstairs they are butchered. I saw blood."

Let me tell you about her urine. Brownish, amber, clear and yellow over the years. Her piss is a pond. Lake Walden. The state measures and weighs Mrs. Myles. The size of her heart, enlarged. They patted her belly. Abdomen was soft and rounded, it reported. RACE: Irish. Which is not the same as white. MAMMARY GLANDS: Atrophic. No matter. Mother of seven, she's got food in the bank. Massachusetts will nurse her, again and again. In 1955 when she has been in Westborough for fifteen years (APPETITE: Normal, SLEEP: Normal. Patient is ambulant. SPEECH: Clear) it mentions under mood and emotion that "Mrs. Myles is resentful at times." To spend the remainder of one's life inside a state mental hospital should yield more positive feelings, Massachusetts felt.

# 2.

The people who sold us our house left one thing. A wooden dresser. It was chestnut-colored. It was styled like the tops of buildings. The wood rose like a cresting wave over the crack of its doors that opened in front to reveal some old coat hangers with paper still on them and a tie. It was in my brother's room.

Before Bridgie was born this was my room. The first bed I ever owned with a little pineapple on each post was right under the window and light flooded in in the morning. There was light before breakfast, there was light always. I was a flower that sipped on light. It was warming me up for the day. I was four when my sister was born and then I began to share and was moved across the hall to a large room with eaves and a single window facing the driveway and another house. Terry was given my little room which became more and more a shrine to his boyness and his value as the years went by. He was seven when he was stricken with appendicitis and it must have been intense for my family when just like Helen he almost died from peritonitis and he had the last rites. My family is so weird. We're like witches or something. I could tell you a story about me flipping a nickel from the bottom of the staircase all the way up the stairs into my mother's bedroom and it landing on its edge on a black missal sitting on her bureau. That really happened and I have a photo to prove it, but my brother's story is even weirder.

Terry, a week before he got sick and almost died, came down to breakfast in the morning before school and said that he had just dreamed that he was dying and the priest was giving him extreme unction and my mother snapped, don't say that. She hates the occult, all signs of superstition horrify her. Anyway, those things did come to pass, but my brother lived so they decorated his room to the nines. Wallpaper with ships, a new wooden desk and a soft green desk blotter with leather edges. A metal calendar that the days clicked by on. He was having this perfect boy world where I had my baby world, and now I'm across the hall in the dark with my sister. When Terry was dying my mother sat on her wing chair and wept. My father was at work. I said, don't cry Mommy. It was my way of being dramatic. She cried even more.

The dresser was standing in Terry's room for years until he took woodworking, and built himself a closet. He just busted into the drying room and took some space. Can we get rid of this dresser. Well, it came with the house, my mother laughed.

It was too large for the halls. Angling and lifting, my parents tried to get it out. I heard Daddy huffing. Squat, stoop, sweating away. Finally they decided to shove it off the roof. That was the idea. There was a little flat roof outside the window. It was pretty out there, the Barkers who gave my mother vegetables had such a nice yard and the roof next door was bright blue. My father stood on ours, having his smoke. Right over there was our chestnut tree. He used to climb up the branches in fall and jounce on them and we'd all gather the spiney things in buckets. We were urged to go downstairs and watch. This was a Saturday morning in the fall. Bridgie remembers it vividly because it was her birthday. He gave the dresser a push. "Here it comes," he yelled. My father falling down. It reminded me of a religious painting. He was hanging so still in the air. Then he sprawled in the gravel like he was asleep. It was a gorgeous fall day. The firetrucks came pouring up the street, our neighbors, everyone came. It was like a parade, people pouring up Swan Place. We're so close to the Center. It was easy to watch. We're right here.

# 3.

It's called alcoholism. It runs in my family. We have a genetic disposition towards it and depression. On Nellie's death certificate, as well as stating that she had an enlarged heart, it says that she was depressed.

So...one March evening, I'm walking down the traintracks with my friends to knock back a few Colt 45s. I could feel the world pushing against its own size that night. Expanding. Like my father who swore he'd never drink because of his father ("slightly deaf, a good provider...happy family") I was adamant. I would not. But playing drunk was cute.

Arm around Lorraine when we were five, revolving around the telephone pole, huge thing, at the corner of our streets, singing our baby hearts out, "Show me the way to go home, *hic*, over land and sea and foam, you will always hear me singing our song...then some adult would walk by and laugh. I hear in the Middle Ages they only had booze on holidays, the whole town got loaded, say for spring or the harvest, and everyone would fuck each other in the hay, and then the booze was all gone and they'd go back to work. I mean I know the kings continued to get drunk, to make history, but the peasants had these gigantic episodes and only that. Who would want to hear about a king?

In Arlington the whole town was drunk. It was the only dry town in the state of Massachusetts. So it was one nice thing a drunk could do for his family, buy a house in Arlington. I walk down those train tracks all my life. Burnt gravel, the future. The pond. It looks strange in retrospect, almost like a stage. The long mound of the empty tracks. The direction to Cambridge, Boston, and out. Dear Mom, I'm gone. Steal horses in Medford, Triple A stables, Texas to get hats. We drew this map. Ate our sandwiches on the tracks. They were covered by jungle on either side—bushes. I was with Patty Delay and Ruthy.

The Delays did it large, introduced me to a world of plant poison. I mean, they were covered in ringworms, bites and sores, one of them, Gracie, had false teeth at fourteen from coasting, no one ever had their eyes poked out, close, and of course they got poison ivy and poison oak. We didn't in my family. We just didn't have it, we were inimitably unlike the Delays. Our dolls were intact, we had no dogs. We read. We went to the library. Our meals were quiet, no one would come wrestling out the screen door, slam, and four others to restrain him, or even better, call the cops. We sat there eating, kind of happy. You could not make our skin blister and itch. No one in my family had ever gotten poison ivy. Yet.

Look, I said to the Delays, and eight lips sneered: Socks with her sneakers, snob! Eileen Myles lifted a greasy branch of the stuff. I will prove it to you. I won't get it. I rubbed shiny leaves on my arms, laughing, I scrubbed it on my cheeks and eyes. They were all watching. I was not like them, it was impossible, the Delays would see. It was absolutely one of the worst cases of poison ivy anyone had ever seen, short of hospitalization. Deep in the bowl of that summer, I was lolling in fumes of yellow soap, thick pink calamine lotion. I was guiltily engaged in fevered scratching, the near-orgasmic itch. My eyes were caked, almost sealed—blind—while huge whirling fans aimed my pitiful way. I was a giraffe. In the afternoon kids came by with old comic books I could barely read so they could see how bad (heh-heh) showoff Myles was.

I am human, I decided. I knew my weakness, like kryptonite, and I could do it again. I was not a bad kid. I always pushed it, but not so far. I had a deal with God. If I failed to do homework, in the absent-minded way, I wouldn't get caught. If I skipped it on purpose, watching teevee, I would get nailed. God protected my spaciness and innocence. We had an understanding that things would essentially go my way if I was generally good. God was fair, God cut me a margin of error. I was safe. Bad kids got caught. I could never afford to get caught. It was sad in my house with my father being dead, and my mother now so totally alone, again, after her enormously sad childhood. Also I must admit there was some lingering mystery around his death, his strange fall off the roof. Sometimes I wondered if she killed him, and maybe she would kill me too. I was afraid of her.

To keep things cool I made utterly sure I was never so bad a nun asked to see my mother. I didn't do much. Laugh and pass notes. And once in a while I drummed.

The wood of our desks was about an inch thick. They were hollow, stuffed with old papers and half pencils, gum wrappers, school smell, and if you slapped the joints of your fingers just below the tips on the band of golden wood that surrounded the absent inkwell you got this low thudding that felt like your whole body got released in that place, it was like drawing, with no pictures, just this oooooooooo strumming nervousness, a sweet sound. The desk played tight like close to the rim of my bongos which no one had ever heard. I had this record by Jack Costanza, Mr. Bongo, and he had a straw hat and a bow tie and a vest and behind him was a long-haired woman with castanets, her head flung back, really beautiful. She was dancing to Jack, and so were the kids in the room when I played. It was a joke, I knew I was being a jerk, but it sounded so good in the empty room, and I was doing my beatnik imitation, eyes closed, and the nun turned around from the board and said, Who is that boy who is banging his thumbs on the desk. I stopped. The room grew silent now. Who is that boy. The curve of the room was so loud. The traffic on Medford Street hummed, the trees were shaking with their teeny green buds practically smiling in the breeze. If everything stopped and I was silent, the nun would give up.

Kids were turning around. Who is that boy. The room was silent. It's Jack, I prayed. It's not me, it's Jack. I was sweating now. Sister would-n't stop. She bellowed. I will keep the whole class after school if that boy will not stand up right now and have the manliness to admit—

I stood up. Everyone hollered and screamed. The boys went Myles. Kids were dying. The girls giggled and blushed. Janet Lukas and Susie were imitating me, silently playing their drums on their desk. I felt so ugly. Tell your mother I want to see her at the convent tomorrow evening. The worst. My mother loves nuns. She wanted to be one. What shall we do about Eileen. The nun and my mother sitting on velvet furniture. I started to try and make a deal, which I always do. I got as close as I could, I whispered. Let me do a punish task, I was practically bowing to her in front of the class, lifting my paws, pulling her dress. I will be perfect, I whined. No, young lady, and she spat lady out like what a joke and the class got it and sneered…Catholic school was choreographed abuse. I've seen, I've heard your kind of perfect. I need to talk to Mrs. Myles, and we'll decide what perfect is for you. I slunk back to my desk. I must do something. My head was bowed. 1962. I had a permanent.

I banged on the Delays' front door. Dickie came to greet me, he was tall and handsome. He was scratching his belly. It was a special confi-dent guy gesture. Dickie was in high school. He had dark red hair. Short. All the girls had crushes on him. He looks like Dr. Kildare, which I couldn't see. He wore grey athletic teeshirts that hung loose-ly from his thin strong frame and Dickie held the door with one hand and scratched his lightly furred belly, with the belly button kind of protruding and you could see the top of his BVDs. For a boy I didn't think was so cute, I memorized every fucking thing. He turned his head yelling loudly into the house. Ruthy. He turned to me quietly and said, she'll be out in a minute. He had something to eat in his hand and he lowered his head and took a bite. He looked at me for a second then he vanished into the dark of the house. I waited a moment. I yelled, Ruthy.

I need poison ivy. I can't go to school tomorrow. You're shitting me. Yes. Ruthy threw her leg over the railing, and then we went over the fence. It was before supper. For years we came home at the six o'clock train. Myles you are nuts she said as I rubbed the shiny leaves on my legs and my arms. It was a suspiciously even-handed attack. Good thing you didn't get it on your face my mother sniffed.

When I think of the early part of my life, everyone, adults were always looking sideways. No one saw me straight on. I was never in the same world with them unless they were really mad. And then it was like for a second. My mother and the nun never sat down one evening on the on the old velvet furniture in the convent. And soon I was eighth grade and these old problems were over.

If you can pick something up, leaves from a bush, and with the juices stop a conversation between some adults, then there's probably even more things in the world like that. Things that make you stop and start. On my brother's birthday I drank a beer. I had always been envious of him. I wanted to be a Terry. To have the name my father had and his father, way on back to Ireland. Because it was so clearly in the name, being a man. You wouldn't be bad for wanting things, then. The riches would all be given to you. You were the hope.

Want another one, Leena. Ferret threw it and I caught. Pop. The beer was tasteless, and yet there was a shimmer around the tiny trees on the tracks and down below the ball field, with lights on poles, the bleachers, all of nature was looking slightly bigger and Gary took my hand. He pushed his big mouth against me. We were kissing outside, this was the first time, and his mouth was wet, but it was simply funny and we didn't laugh because it was so slow, like we were in a dream and I never had this exact one again. Then I went home and ate cake. Terry was 16 and blew the candles out. We applauded and my mother turned on the light. I gave him a zippo and he went flick. *That's* not so good, said my mother. Terry and I grinned. Thanks Leena.

# 4.

When I first sat in a church basement, and I was no longer drinking, I had this one thought. I would say it often and everyone would laugh. I don't understand, I would say, I was twelve years old and I wanted to be an astronaut, and then I was sitting here. Heh-heh the room would go. I was this kid. Studiously watching teevee shows about space travel and movies, and I read science fiction and I would carefully observe just what kind of people were welcomed on rocket ships. We knew that you would sit in chairs that spun real fast and see how many g's you could take. G means gravity. I could take a lot of g's, I knew that. But to get on the ship you needed some other kind of skill. So for a time I would be a geologist, I would learn about rocks. There would certainly be weather on the moon or Mars. Meteorology. I would look at those buffoons on teevee who only got as far as the five o'clock news. You could go a lot further with weather. Or an ordinary doctor might be welcomed aboard. So for years medicine was a cover for the larger space travel goal. It took the heat off. Eileen wants to be a doctor, Aunt Gladys. The Delays offered this bit of information to their schoolteacher aunt who lived near the park where we played in the summer. She was the nice part of their family, and so they offered her my ambition as pleasant car talk. I could be useful. Is that so you can help people dear, said Aunt Gladys, her carefully driving head slightly turned. Gladys's hair was prematurely white. Eerie. This solitary teacher, a witch. I looked at my feet. I want to go to the moon, I thought. I just ignored her. She would never understand. Aunt Gladys is talking to you, said Ruthy. Who had bright red hair. She looked like a rabbit when she got mad. Her lip and nose sneered together into a rodent place. It was air-conditioned inside Aunt Gladys's car. The witch's ship. Yup, I said to everything. Uh-huh, I said to the world. Guess so. Everything a girl did was supposed to be good. Aunt Gladys was a dyke.

Our park was mentioned in Paul Revere's ride. Menotomy Rocks Park. After the Old Men of Menotomy, but "monotony" was the joke. The park was large with lots of trees and Hills Pond, where I caught a fish, and it was the happiest moment of my life. On younger trips to Monotony, seven or eight of us would trot over, as horses, and once we passed the tall wrought iron gates we'd run up the dirt path to the water fountain. It had a base of cement, with a cement stem and a bowl with a metal spout. We had this race every day and one day I won. I tripped on the last step. I went face first into the fountain and cracked my front tooth.

But I want to talk about Mars. Where my family came from. I wanted to roll in its warm red sands like a dog. I wasn't sure I believed in the canals. I was aware of the theories of Schiaparelli. But, 47,000,000 miles away, the eyes can deceive. I loved the portraits of the lonely men who had charted outer space for us. Tycho Brahe with his funny hat, his arms folded across his chest. Behind him the incredibly huge telescope in his medieval planetarium. Alone in his castle he conceived of outer space. I never could decide if I wanted to look or go. Obviously the astronomers were the lookers and I was a looker too. It was such a gorgeous dream, the universe whirling around. Purple little Venus with her gassy climate, and strange reptiles slithering through the planet-wide swamp that textured this cloudy planet smelling so strongly of ammonia. I wanted to smell it! To be there too! To lie on a hot rock covered in seaweed, wearing the necessary gas mask, oh to look back at the monstrous gleaming face of the Sun from only 10 million miles away. Venus *is* music, that's the feeling I always had. In that swampy goo of early civilization dawning, a low tone vibrates, a tiny ooooooh emanating from the particular combination of vapors and plankton and plain old heat, sometimes it seemed possible that the sound created the planet, those steamy conditions, rather than the other way around.

I bet you never heard of Vulcan. That was my favorite thing. An early Polish astronomer, Pierscienewicz, cited a tiny tiny planet, not an asteroid, but a planet, a sphere fulfilling all the elliptical characteristics of planetary solar revolutions, and it was even closer than Mercury to the sun. I never cared much about Mercury. But Vulcan was of particular interest to me because this one scientist had spotted it, and then there were a smattering of other reports during the mid-seventeenth century, of a teeny orange planet going around and around. There are no twentieth century sightings of Vulcan, none at all. Mainly it's the seventeenth century that harbored the Baroque notion that if you think Mercury's hot, we've got something even smaller faster and hotter for you, this clanging fierce-armed god of liquid fire. For me this planet practically had ears, it was the devil, or something really wild.

Because I suspected I was the only 20th century enthusiast of this planet, I treasured this spot in the solar system, even if it was now blank. What could have happened to my little planet. Tumbled into the inferno of our solar system, just fell off its axis or something, cracked down the middle from the heat of the sun, and maybe two pieces of Vulcan broke into four then sixteen. Perhaps a huge lick of the sun's tongue picked up poor Vulcan and flung him into the orbit of another planet, not exactly, but maybe in the neighborhood of Jupiter and Mars, becoming those not very interesting pieces of space dust, the asteroids.

I pulled a number two pencil off my night table and I did something I never do. See I have a total reverence for books. Maybe once on a library book I got really nervous. I think I went crazy. You're not supposed to get a library book dirty in any way, so I took a ballpoint pen and scribbled like crazy, then closed it instantly, feeling sick. Then I repaired it thoughtfully. Got a very soft eraser and gently went over the spot, rubbing. I got most of it out, and then it was due. I slid it onto the librarian's desk with a sense that this could be the end of my membership to my favorite place in the world, the best smelling, the most private, the most exciting. I have to tell you there's something about the library that always made me so happy I had to take a tremendous dump. Sometimes I had to run home, if some other kid was in there. I looked around and everywhere I could see there were more books, they would never run out, and it was free and it was quiet and I belonged. Smash. I threw my book down and ran to the toilet.

The children's library smelled different. I remember that.

But let me tell you about the book I owned. My special secret about Vulcan. It was a Collier's Junior Classic, no. 6, Greek & Roman Myths. I took a yellow pencil and I wrote carefully on the page that's glued to the inside of the book, before the book starts, and there was some uniform design there that was on the inside of all the volumes of this beautiful set of books that I owned. I wrote the secret of Vulcan, my loyalty to this planet, and the manner in which my tiny orange planet came to its end. I knew that someday I would be a famous scientist and they would find my books from my childhood and it would be incredible that even as a child she was thinking so much about science and had discovered something, the death of a planet. Later on I grew ashamed. That very same year, and I erased my theory, but it's there in the book, you can see the smudge and faintly make out the word "Vulcan."

Let me rip through the rest of the solar system while we're there. My grandmother died when I was seven. I imagine my little body sitting in school in the classroom that had its own special effects. Some days the sounds of the rulers and the chalk and the nun's voice would go all funny, like a rumbling beneath it. It was like I was going deaf. It became a dream, school, the regularity of our uniforms, the nun's habit, everything conspired to be regular, but in fact it wasn't. It was simply untrue, a momentary dream world, and I knew this sitting some days in school when everything echoed and wiggled and I was alone.

The Solar System, by Eileen Myles. Mercury, as we've mentioned, is a bore. Tiny, yellowish green. No characteristics, too hot for plant life. Maybe in about a million years when the sun cools down it will become fertile. Today, zilch.

Earth, blue. Blue and brown which are good colors to wear on this planet. Standing on Earth you think the color of the universe is blue, but it is not. It doesn't have a color. Color is a toy for people on this planet. They see everything in terms of it. Their heart would be broken if they knew it didn't exist. For instance it's not so odd that the greatest astronomers in history are from Poland and Italy. Especially Italy. Have you been there? There's a richness of landscape, and the beautiful red food (pasta) and of course the people are better looking than people anywhere in the world, and if you enjoy the Italian painting which I do, then it's clear you're kind of standing at the butthole of the illusion of beauty on the human planet, Earth, and from Italy they're so happy they even look at the sky, and enjoy the stars and eventually they aimed and focused their telescopes and discovered the planets. There's something loungey about the Poles as well. They have great legs. They love art, that's just a fact, and somehow art and astronomy are right next to each other, not just in the alphabet, but if your eye is hungry for God, for seeing him and you know you never will, there's this longing you live with in the light of the day and at night you find it in the stars, this sadness you know and you want to go home. They say when you die you move towards the light, and I say what else is new. I mean, are we on the same planet? I'll do a few more.

I think I did Earth. The waves splash. The nicest thing about the Earth is the sea. It's kind of like the sun, but it's wet. Gulls fly above the ocean. It recedes and everything that was covered, rocks and sticks and thousands of pebbles, sits there in the drool of the Earth's mouth, is momentarily exposed, it's like it's drawing its breath. It has moods, it has emotions, the Earth…I mean the sea does. It's kind of like a mirror. Echoes the heavens, absolutely the Moon, so if you want to know what's going on on the Moon, look at the Earth. The Earth is like New York. If you watch too closely, you'll forget everything you ever learned. Everything you know. It's busy, but there's nothing. So if you want to see nothing, look at the Moon. It is nothing. Which I like a lot. People are always comparing things to the Moon. I do it too. Like the back of my house. People compare asses to moons. Every big white face. But the Moon is emptier than that. It's reflective stone. It's like an altar flying through space, one without ritual, just going around and around. I keep changing my mind about whether the men who went there disturbed the Moon's privacy. Nobody cares about that. I do.

Jupiter's huge. We know that. It crams Earth and Moon into one, and maybe Mars too. It's a complicated female planet with that big red dot that expands. There are storms on the surface of the planet, and they're "real storms," and the topography of the planet is constantly changing shape, as the energy of the storm shifts, the picture shifts and the red dot vanishes, and expands accordingly. It's my planet in some way, it's the one that survived. Yet one doesn't want to own a big present and available planet in the same way you might want to possess a tiny little absent planet from at least two centuries ago. Jupiter's getting colder and that's a problem. It's huge and it's never known what to do with its energy. I just want to point out that Earth scientists sometimes suggest that female humans formerly had an estrus cycle like dogs, a period of rut, not a life of periods, as we call menstruation, and it helped the human female protect herself, that is she didn't, it was like the peasant drinking party of the Middle Ages. A big blow-out. Everyone knew what a woman was in the past. When she saw red, she was red. Now it's too complicated on Earth, and it's extremely complicated on Jupiter. One simply has to submit to its size (while you're flying by) and admit that it's changing, and it must and there isn't another way for Jupiter to be. We are currently waiting for more information. Meanwhile she has moons. Definitely not planets, or empty gourds like the Earth's moon. Callisto is sad, Ganymede is frothy and solitary, Io is condemned to be a cloud, and so on. There's at least a dozen, and none are exactly the same, the measurements vary.

Uranus and Neptune are both green. They have similarities but Uranus is the colder of the two, and Neptune is largely inhabited by filmmakers. Pluto is a dark red brown, an icy clot of a planet, that is currently on the move, and that's probably why I'm remembering Vulcan. Last time Pluto turned this way, Vulcan was hot, I mean on the map and with Pluto lining up, though I don't think we'll be exactly putting the cinders of the poor planet back together again, cause once you're an asteroid you're on another track, but all that Vulcan once stood for, Pluto brings, though coldly, and part of the reason Vulcan didn't survive, was too much heat, so Pluto is holding a bowl of ideas that were formerly tropical, like ice cream and fruit. Just because dessert comes at the end (like Pluto) doesn't mean it's the end of the meal. It might be the meaning. That's about all I can tell you about the solar system.

# 5.

There are a number of inconsistencies in the report Massachusetts mailed me. The most obvious one is the spelling of the name of the institution: Westborough. The silent "ugh" at the end of the word appears and vanishes throughout the records. The "ugh"is finally excised from Westboro on Nellie's death certificate. And there are many factual errors—small ones and large ones—about my family in these records.

It reminds me of a conversation I once had with my dad. I asked him why my brother wasn't a third. Like Terrence Myles, the third. We couldn't do that he said because my name isn't the same as my father's. In these records it is. They're both Terrance with an *a*. I hate that, I said. I don't like that *a*. I don't like it either, he said. And took a drag of his cigarette.

The time we spoke about this was at the cemetery to see Grandpa's grave. The stone said "Terrance Myles." Like Lombard Terrace. I said to my father. Yeah, he agreed. Lombard Terrance and he made a face. He was funny. My parents didn't want me to be a Junior, he said. We didn't want to do that to your brother either. Oh, I said. I looked at my dad's red face, the crummy grass around grandpa's grave. My father putting his cigarette out with the tip of his black shoe. There was no story. So he's Terrence Frances, and I'm Terrence Joseph.

I wrote my own name on a pad a of paper. Eileen backwards is Nellie. If you turn one of the *e*'s into an *l*. I wonder how he felt about his mother's body. It's all these names and titles with men, yet they pass through a woman's flesh. There are lots of strange things in her records. A million lapses and pauses like poetry. The State tells the epic of the peoples' lives, putting people on the scale, weighing all the wrong things, then acting ponderous about the misinformation. Erasing months and years, but giving what smidgeons of information it does offer as if everything's in order, say the Mental annual Report, 1955, then the physical Annual Report 1955, then just Mental five years later, Physical, in two more years, then the patient's dead. You're supposed to look at all these absences, and feel complete. You're supposed to look at the records like my mother and say, Oh Eileen, there were just so many. Bodies? Women?

Patients, she meant. Nellie was old, she said, irritated. How could we have expected Massachusetts to care, was the implication, yet Massachusetts is so formal in its not caring. Doesn't it ever just go crazy and scrawl, "old fucking piece of shit nobody cares," pouring bile on everything, knowing full well that nobody reads the damn records, everyone's pretending there's an order and a symmetry to the way a bag of female human gets stored away for the rest of her life. Someone, a servant or a college student, will be paid a hundred bucks a week to look at her. Now and then a nurse would write "patient should not be moved. Seems happy here." Another note two months later says that patient was moved to Childs Upper, and then moved again. The nurse's caring seems cruel. It singled Nellie out for a moment, as if it were a real life.

One in which someone looked at the old fidgety white woman and said, "Mum." It's so undone. The feeling is edited away by the state, I see the tiny ellipses and I just feel numb. Her right arm appeared bruised in 1942, and finally they reported that yes, she had a fractured radius. How? Why? Nellie Riordan Myles is at the desk with me. I pat the manila envelope, then I push it away.

I won't write the scenario—a day inside the house of the family Myles, on 273 Washington Street, in Somerville, Mass., St. Joseph's Parish, a typical day in 1939 or 1940, before she went away. She had a "responsible prematurely white-haired son", and an unemployed 23-year-old. She had a daughter who had big features like me. One partially deaf little husband. Who my mother thinks screwed around. All the white legs in the kitchen in the morning. People laughing, maybe seven of them. Twelve legs, John's still in bed, dark and grouchy. He does have a job. So does Helen. Would it be any different if Helen had lived? There's a small mention of Nellie being briefly admitted to a private hospital while Helen was alive. My mother tells me that my grandfather probably didn't want to pay for his wife. The state of course took everything when he died, so he did wind up footing the bill. He was a mean one, said my mother. Oh, she huffs. Sending money back to Ireland all those years when he had six kids. The Myleses were poor. They were always moving and I think that's why. Couldn't pay the rent. Yup, the state took it all, sighed my mother. And, of course, there was nothing for us.

The records mention that Nellie's son, Vincent, died in high school at age 15. Which is definitely not true. I've told you about my Uncle Vin who was digging a hole in Brockton, Mass. in approximately 1960. Easily twenty-five years after his alleged death. He was also at breakfast this morning. Why would the state tell this lie. It didn't. Probably while Ted and Edward were being interviewed in the hospital office someone dropped a chart, a truck backed up outside and the intake person thought they said that Vincent died. Or someone died, they knew that. In many ways, the state's pictures of my family are no more erratic and conventional than our own. Sundays arranged with great formality. All of us standing around my beautiful grandmother, her sitting, with the sun in our eyes. If I could circle that formation, walk around with a camera, get us from the back or the side. It might begin to seem noble, somehow. The Myleses staring ahead, in profile. The rumpled grass-stained derriere of the Myles family. A portion of

Nellie's kerchiefed head from behind. The small foot of one us—
Bridgid's foot, curled around her other shoe. What's strange is that
these *are* the portraits of my family, topped only slightly by our days at
the beach.

The institution was true. It was our Buckingham Palace, we paid for
it, and it was the place where we returned. Terry and I cheerfully sat
on the stone steps of the hospital, or were jumping in the tulips,
rolling down hills. Dad went inside. My mother stayed out with us and
the camera. Nellie is led out with great aplomb. The queen mother.
The camera clicks. All I can add, what I contain, is a memory of the
texture of her skin, how soft it was when I kissed her cheek. Her skin
was cool—old and sweet. She was happy when she saw me, because I
was a baby, I was life.

My father came out of Nellie. That's how it works, the baby was
squeezed out, by her tired muscles, and probably at home. She was a
thirty-seven-year-old woman when my father was born. It was like
friends of mine, who know they can have another, though it might not
be a great idea. To spread your legs as a female. To let someone squirm
out. The most adult girl in junior high, well maybe the loudest, was
telling a story once—she was laughing at her mother, at her own
moment of birth. Debbie heaved with delight. "She ran to the phone,
a baby hanging out of her ass—." We all sat in silence. Then someone
told her. Debbie, babies don't come out of your ass.

What do you mean, she laughed, of course they do. She looked at us.
I shook my head. Everyone did. Where do they come from, goaded
Debbie, humoring us. I pointed between my legs. Really?

How could someone come out of me, my cunt, someone alive? You
travel through the warm tunnel of your mother. You lay on her bush,
her belly. Mom. You suck on her teat. Maybe. You grab her leg for
years, the part that's as tall as you. She gives you food. She makes you
eat. You throw it around. She puts food in a bag and hands it to you.
You go into the world. Come home and she's there. She touches the

back of your head. Even as an adult. This woman has permission to put food in your mouth. She tugs on your clothes. Then one day you walk in the house, her house, and it's empty. Mum's gone. She's out, and when she returns she's got a different look. She was just talking with her friend. And everything's okay, it's good. She begins to cook dinner. Her strength is what makes the world safe. The mother at the stove. In her house. My mother turning the light out. The heated child body, the sick child is tended by her. The humming of her voice, the song she sings while she's waiting for her kid to get up. She taught me to pray. She has struck me several times. My mother enforces the clock. As the temperature changes she hands me clothes. The food warms and cools as the earth turns slowly through the year. My mother is time. She hands it to me.

Nellie begins to go outside at night with nothing on and calls her daughter's name again and again. Her girl is dead. The panic rises in a young man's body when the whiteness of the body, Mum, she's an old woman, has to be dragged in and put in her bed like a child. Or it's winter and she wears a hat. It's the middle of summer, June, and it's light out and all the neighbors see Nellie with her coat and her stockings down around her ankles, and her slippers on and Edward drags her in. Mum, he goes, and the door slams.

Teddy's outside. The one who smokes. You okay Ted? He shrugs. 23. It's before the war. I don't know this man. He's handsome. I sit with his little square face on my desk. A photo booth shot I snagged at home. There's no one there but my mom. She won't miss his mouth, big eyebrows and deep penetrating eyes. Large nose. Kind of shy-looking, though. Slightly criminal. It's true. My dad has lost his clock. How's Nellie asks the neighbor. She's up at the hospital. The neighbor shakes his head. Night Ted, and walks up Washington Street. The mother's body, a vulnerable thing, a hearth. Open the wrong door. The white shock of it. She's sick and the family steps around quiet, waiting for day to return. Her sweaty head on a pillow. Thanks when you give her some tea. My father's clock is broken. He threw it down a well. And the baby took a wife.

# 6.

Vincent's wife was Aunt Marie. We didn't see them much as they lived on the South Shore in a modern house. I wanted to live in one of those. There were a bunch on Memorial Drive in Cambridge. Big triangles of glass and reddish brown wood and sometimes there'd be panes of color too, and you knew that inside they could watch the world, cars passing and trees. I don't know what Vincent did, but he made more money than you did at the Post Office. He had gone to a little bit of college. But he seemed like a child. He was quiet. He had pretty eyes. Everyone called him Vinnie. Especially Marie, who had black hair and sat on the curved white couch. They had two kids, Vinnie and Debbie. When Vincent died, which was not too long after my father, Marie remarried a hockey coach. That was quick. The kids probably took his name says my mother. They're about 40. My cousin Vinnie was last seen wearing a striped teeshirt shorts and sneakers. He had freckles. Debbie was pretty, darker hair. White teeshirt little pink trim and pink shorts. Marie hit her once in front of everyone, and her ring cut the kid. Blood on little Debbie's face. Red sneakers. I remember us all standing in the garage. My parents had a lot invested in disliking Marie. She had a bouffant bubble like Annette Funicello. She wore tight capris and read movie magazines and ate chocolates. Marie loves wine, said my mother as if that were a crime. My father once called her a dago sexpot. *Ted*, my mother said.

Someone asked me once if it was bad in my house. I said it wasn't supposed to be. That's the real answer. It was a fake state we lived in for years. The more something was going on, the more we ignored it, hoped we were wrong. Marie pushed Vinnie. It was a phenomenon I saw more in my friends' families than ours. The guy was usually from Somerville, Irish, a regular guy, a drunk. If the wife was something slightly different, say a wasp or even Italian like Marie, you'd see her insist the guy go to law school nights, drink beer, not whiskey. She'd move him along. He'd be wearing a suit. You'd walk in the house and meet this sad-eyed guy and this irritated woman who didn't like me hanging around with her kid. I always knew I looked wrong. Marie knew it. And I had such a crush. My mother and Aunt Marie would be talking in the kitchen and I would sit on her big white couch that went around the enormous teevee and I'd clip a chocolate and throw myself down with an issue of *Photoplay*. Marie was so cool. This is exactly how I want to live when I grow up. Eileen, yelled my mother. Are you having any lunch. The world began in the kitchen.

In my house there were generally paper napkins, scrunched up in your hand during dinner, all sticky next to your plate or probably on the floor or between your legs but certainly not on your lap. My mother didn't pay much attention to us. We were everyone, this thing she served, and I was eating alone. Terry was a lefty. It was the only thing planned. He sat there and I always sat here. I set the table. Because I was a girl. It took them years to get me this far. Upright. There used to be a little window seat at the table. It was mine. I'd lie down on its cold red cushions with buttons and I could see the tree. My family would be clattering their plates above my head and I was very happy down there. Neither boy, nor girl. Eat Eileen. To be dragged upright to do this boring thing. Eat. With everyone. And I was simply light. Leaves blinking in the chestnut tree. They took my seat away. Okay—that moment is past.

Aunt Marie was wild about Terry. Ugh. Terry, the good boy, totally charming adults, especially women. He looked like the perfect little son. I don't know what he said or did, but I arrived at the table and he'd already said something brilliant. And now I was supposed to start eating. Like I had been there all along and was so happy. I ate my pickles. I picked up my sandwich. I looked around. My mother, who couldn't stand Aunt Marie, was smiling and laughing. My brother was eating like a pig and being special. He kept ramming his fat hands into the potato chip bowl. Marie was calling my mother Gen, her special way so it rhymed with pin, it sounded more tinny in Marie's mouth. My father and Vincent are outside digging a hole. I am totally serious. They are out in the yard at this moment. If the men were in the kitchen I would have felt safe.

They were all fake friends, my brother showing off and my mother and Marie's high voices. I couldn't bite. I just couldn't imagine pushing my teeth through the bread. I put it down on the plate. I just wasn't nice. I hated them. I felt hot. I wanted to lie down on my window seat. I was around ten. I was in a sweatshirt. Marie was one of those women who hated me because I wasn't a girl. That was my horrible secret. My mother looked at me nervously. C'mon, Dear, eat your sandwich. She had that teeny edge in her voice, it was musical but nervous. I was embarrassing her. Catch up, the voice said. You are not my girl.

I picked up my sandwich. I felt so alone in Aunt Marie's kitchen. Can I go outside. No, finish your sandwich. I knew I couldn't do it. I couldn't chew. It was old turkey, from yesterday. I think because my mother didn't like Marie, she couldn't have me not eating Marie's food. I made everything obvious. My mouth wouldn't work. It couldn't smile, it couldn't talk, it couldn't bite. I could hear the clank of shovels. My father had his back to us. I could see them outside. Goofing around, having a smoke. Men just had to pretend to work. It was how they played. Women had to pretend to like each other. I felt so huge. The rubber turkey, and my teeth like joke teeth, that couldn't bite. The bread would break, the meat hanging out of my mouth, white meat and fat, mayonnaise, and my mother kept looking at me, and Marie kept turning her head away and it was so hard that my mother had such an ugly daughter. I could be her success. I'm not. I wanted to cry but I was even too dry for that. I want my dad. Can I go outside. Yes. Please. Get out of my sight.

# 7.

On one side of Swan Place there's a tall apartment building...not that
tall really. Just big and wide and bricks and stuff. There used to be a
huge field and a house there—tan with dark brown shutters. It's funny,
I never cared about that house, don't even remember it unless I'm
climbing over the fence in my head to shag a ball and I see the brown
house that's gone. The field around it had vines with purple grapes and
there were pear trees. I gasped as I went over. I had never seen anything like this. It was like a museum. Maybe once the game was like to
go steal grapes but we got in trouble so fast, because stealing is a crime.
Private property, said the Delays, and we knew we couldn't go there.
There were one-family houses and two-family houses on my street.
Ours was a two. After Lobrino we rented to young couples. Like Pat
and Joe, Joe was actually an Aulenbach, and they had a baby and then
they had two, and at two they moved. Which happened once or twice.
Wish we could find somebody like Lobrino, my mother said. Because
Mrs. Lobrino didn't die, you know. She moved to the Cape. That's
what you do in Massachusetts. So we found those women.

I think we just placed an ad, maybe in the *Advocate*, and my father was
home sick and the women called and he showed them the place and he
called my mother at work and she said, up to you Ted, so we rented to
them. I bet this was about 1960. They were women in their thirties.
One of them was tall. She wore cat's-eye glasses and had a permanent,
and she wore a sweatshirt and jeans like me and she stayed home in the

day and didn't go to work. She painted. Seemed like we had a beatnik downstairs. Her name was Kim. I should have liked her, but she made me sick. The other woman went to work. Her name was Mildred, Mildred Patterson. Her hair was grey and she pushed it back over her ears, they called it a DA, and she wore car coats, which were short, covered your ass, but were good for driving. I guess you don't want to sit on your jacket when you drive. Mildred drove to work. She worked for her father who was a teevee repairman.

At this time in history the person who fixed your teevee would come to your home. It made our house much more a part of the world that these important services could take place there, that people would come for these purposes. It meant the teevee was part of the family. And when you died the priest would come, and of course the doctor would come too.

I had a large drawing pad and that Christmas while we were waiting for my father to come home and my mother was crying I decided to lie down on the rug in front of the teevee and draw the tree. I began. It was definitely the same year the women moved in and I was putting each needle on one by one with my charcoal pencil and I felt everything would be fine when I was done.

My father wanted me to go downstairs and see Kim's art. I didn't want to. Kim made us a wreath once for our door. It was Mylar maybe. It was reddish green and kind of ugly and reflective, and it made noise when it shook. Not real loud but a faint kind of rustle. I had to go downstairs and get it. It was so close, the apartment downstairs, but still it felt like another world. The hollow of the staircase and my feet thumping down on the rug. There was a click and a ga-gung to the door, almost a song in the middle of everything, eighteen years I lived in that house. I looked up and there was this big woman swaying trying to put the wreath on our door with a piece of tape. She almost fell. I felt sick. She was constantly smiling, and I was standing in that little hallway room with her, and once it stuck, I could get away. Ga-gung and run upstairs. Well, what is it said my mother. Wreath, I said, already reading the paper. I could hear the taps of supper and I liked to stay close. It's on the door, I said.

My mother adjusted everything on the stove one more time and went quietly down to see what's what. Ga-gung she was back. She made a quick face at me, who was still reading the comics on the couch. She was silent like they'd hear. Her face said, big deal. She was not very impressed by those ladies but at least they wouldn't have kids.

The apartment downstairs was cold. The red floors without rugs felt empty. It was a little apartment for people starting a life. Kim was showing me her paintings. The big moment had come. It was a lighthouse, done in grey oils. It looked crooked. It really wasn't great. My father kept saying I should do this. To meet a real painter would be good. She was swaying, and I think she asked me if I wanted a Coke and I said no and she didn't hear me and opened the refrigerator but there wasn't one. Do you want a banana? She kept saying my name. Very carefully, like I would take her seriously if she knew I was Eileen. I think there was a painting of cats. I want you to take one, she grinned. It's okay, I said. Look at all these, she was pointing to them piled in the corners and behind the doors. All lousy. I left with one, a big crooked lighthouse. Let me see, said my mother. I turned it for a second and I made a face. She sighed and returned to the stove. They're artists, she sang. Dinner was huffing.

After dinner one night it got bad. We heard this banging downstairs, like banging on the wall. The door opened for a moment, and someone started to go out the front door then someone pulled them back in. Yelling and crashing. I don't remember too well. Girls, girls my mother said, in her softly chiding voice when she went downstairs into the tiny hall. There was sobbing. I can't have this. The door slammed. No, no, said my mother. This was her house. You do not close the door in her face. We couldn't even close the doors in our rooms. She tried to get my father who was lying on my parents' bed. Oh you're no good, my mother said. He was drunk. She went back down. No, no, no. Her voice was panicky, like she was talking to a pet. The animal was no good, but my mother must keep her dignity. She did.

Ted, she screamed up when she was standing on our stairs. My father wasn't listening either. Ted, if I had ever known when we rented to those two women. We evicted them. It was so easy. They just had to go. There were lots of paintings lying in the trash. Sneakers and some sweatshirts. They left really fast. So what was going on down there, Mom, I asked her a couple of years later. They were a couple of love-birds, she said. We thought it was a good idea, two women. It looked good. They wouldn't leave us. She laughed at herself. I think your father liked to go down and have a drink with Kim. That was his idea. He never missed a trick. She smiled and shook her head.

# 8.

My mother's best friend was her sister. At five o'clock they'd have their cocktail hour. My mother's chair was snug to the wall, dinner was on, and her Manhattan sat on a small table to her right. She was holding a Kent. I loved my mother smoking. Eileen will you go and see if those potatoes are boiling over. I never knew what I'd do if they were, and they weren't. Hmmm, huh. My mother's eyes rolled around the room. I think she liked me lying there on the couch in the den, my head as close as it could get to her talk, her half of the conversation. Occasionally a Polish word would sputter from her lips. Her eyes would light wildly at those moments, and water, just the pleasure of going to that ancient place with her sister Anne. They grew up in East Cambridge in an entirely Polish neighborhood, learned Polish history in school, said their prayers in Polish, ate Polish food, the only remnant of that moment in our lives were the curious and inevitable galunkies, stuffed cabbage rolls. Kind of greasy light green with bloody red peppers holding everything together, a toothpick too, and a handful of orange-stained rice spilled out when your fork met the green wad.

My family was split, the Irish relatives were withholding and sarcastic, drinkers, different kinds, and because they mostly were male, my Irish relatives carried that message that being Irish was right, or normal or something, and there was something female and laughable, and more off the boat to be Polish, I guess speaking another language made them of another land. Poland had been a really big country before the war. She would toss this off as a casual fact that she had learned in school, but it was sad nonetheless that Poland used to be big and we threw that into the odd lot of things we knew about ourselves, our ancestry in a country that was mostly gone. Poland made us a bit different from the kids in school, in that snobby small way—that you weren't Irish or Italian like everyone at St. Agnes but something else. In the distant past, the Nellie years, when my family had a lot of strange tentacles, we'd go to a big city named Lawrence in another part of the state and a man named Judga Tony with a soft hat and a woman named Chorcha Ann would smile and hardly be able to speak to us and their faces were brown and leathery and Chorcha had a gold tooth and when you arrived at their home which was under an El with a store that had a shoe on its sign nearby you'd go up an entirely different smelling set of stairs and food would be laid out, lots and lots of food and the people smiled at us, and patted us and we were supposed to eat. Poles liked food, that was a fact, and my mother would talk about food on the phone with her sister, did she get that eye of the round at Johnnie's? You went to Waltham. Anything good?

I liked the bands of the day around 1957, '58 and '59. Comforting. A spoon stirring. A stripe beginning with breakfast, oatmeal would begin the movie I knew as my life, soon I'd be sipping milk in school, small bottles, clink, potato chips before lunch, my box clanking open to a baloney sandwich, standing with our bellies sticking out in prayer, poetry recitation, pledge of allegiance and down to sleepy math, and diagramming sentences, bells prayer and home to put on real clothes. To play, then lie around waiting for dinner, while my mother talked on the phone. People were losing their teeth, people were dying, having ulcers, people had their butts repaired by a special doctor, people gambled away the candy store, took those pills, worked for their goddamn uncle, the car won't start, Ted cracked one up, the phone was black. Yes he is. My father was on the other couch. Yes, Anne. Yes. Feeling around. My mother's eyes would get teary. Eileen don't you have anything better to do than watching me. Adults never wanted me to see them. I had to wait for my friends to die to look at them a lot. By then I was really thirsty.

My mother's eyes got moist and I had to go away. I go in the parlor and put on a record. I like to hear the same song again and again. I like to read the same poem. I like to sleep with the same person. The more the day looks the same the more I feel good. My mother said she had to kiss her mother goodbye. She was four. She had to stand on her tippy toes and kiss the ice cold face of her mother. Her dress was blue, said my godmother. Oh I don't remember that. My mother's eyes get teary. Yes, my godmother brightens, and she wore white shoes. I don't remember that at all. Oh my god Gen she had so many clothes. My mother's shaking her head. I kissed her cold dead face. She has that one little story going around and around. Her mother was a small woman, but she was very charming, she had a big personality.

I don't remember this. My godmother goes on and on about a woman named Anna, a waitress who died around 1925 who had so many shoes. Gen, you don't remember your mother. My mother's smiling, I don't, she looks at me and laughs, she sniffs. I don't. And her eyes are wet.

The last time I saw my aunt was on Christmas Eve, 1992. The day before I went to the Brooklyn Museum with a friend and the gift shop was selling these light plastic balls for a tree. They were orbs, silver and gold and metallic blue. There was a smaller size, like the clenched fist of a child of five, another the size of an infant's head, say eighteen months. All round things seem like planets and people. When I started working in stores, I worked at the Harvard Coop and it was the sixties and the world contained lots of large shiny things. The world was pulsating and I was making money. A Christmas tree is the prettiest thing I know. It's like every kind of art, it's my model for genius.

You start with nature and build upon it with lights and orbs that echo the brightness, and the tinsel resembles icicles, streams of gas in outer space. Aunt Anne's tree was a serious effort. My aunt revealed her character on holidays. Her small house was huge, plates of food because she was Polish, plus Christmas music playing nonstop, loads of booze. I had my first official drink and cigarette there at 15. Look at this picture. My sweater was burnt orange, cable knit, a cardigan. My teenage eyes half closed, a cigarette nervously lifted to my lips and some extended arm from outside of the frame, my cousin with his lighter, getting me started. I hold a goblet of golden beer in my other hand. Across the room is the deeper occasion, Aunt Anne's massive tree. She used angel hair. It was spun glass that looked like cotton candy. It swirled through the dark green branches and when I was very young I had to be continually shooed away like a little dog. At Christmas a child is never alone.

I thought her name was Aunt Dan. The *T* pushed the oncoming *A* like a *D*. The pause is like a push, or a *tsk* and I'm sure it has its roots in Polish. Aunt Dan was like Adrien, Sandy or Lee, a name that means person, not woman or man. She was the most feminine of women, and she had only sons. She was a little power house, chasing her sister through her life, guiding and urging, basically telling my mother what to do. My mother was whiney. I would say their relationship was the rock of both their lives, their sisterly push-pull defining home for us, the irritation my mother felt indicating the enormity of her dependence on her sister. Oh Anne she'd say when she got off the phone. She'd wave her hand in a gesture of frustration that would only be heightened and intensified by the children leaving home, the loss of each of their husbands, the sisters' bond becoming life itself, it's clatter, a point made silently by the years that followed Anne's death and the weighty absence of that joining gesture, the morning telephone call Anne made to my mother—always at 10:30, no words, or else: *You're not supposed to pick up*! Well how are you?

I plucked a big gold ball for Aunt Anne, a giant earring, a bauble like dyed hair, like her huge personality, her insistence that we sit together on holidays with our galliano drinks, our crème de menthes and our beers, and sing the twelve days of Christmas, and no one ever crossed Anne, she didn't intimidate you, she just convinced you with her radiant smile that it would be fun for you. And it was. Because Aunt Anne was sexy. She believed in family and anyone could come.

I didn't mind the drunks, because most of my family was drunk. But I couldn't bear the priests and the brothers, the endless homosexuals who came around in their stupid cabana sets, in the summer, or a young single woman such as June, who didn't have a mom. June was Aunt Anne's ceramics teacher. Thanks to June, Aunt Anne made Pinky and Blue Boy lamps and Madonna plant holders with praying hands. If you graduated from high school you would get a shiny graduation statue with a pen holder and your name in script and the date of your departure from grade school, or college. All of our moments meant something to Aunt Anne. It was like she was an airport and we were her planes. How she saw us!

Anne and Tim had moved out of Somerville, and Tim had been dead for a few years now, and Anne owned a small "single" in Medford, and my mother groaned at all of Anne's affectations around finally having acquired a house of her own and some property, a yard. Medford is close to Arlington.

You drove here by yourself? Without your mother? I nodded. It's good to see you kid, she said toughly. We kissed and then we sat down and had a cup of tea. I handed her the box and she pulled out that bauble. It reflected me.

Well that's nice, she said and smiled. No word from your sister. None, I said. Bridgid had left my family five years before. I was glad I was here. My gift had been absorbed into the atmosphere, which was the grandeur of her death, so close and we both knew.

I want to talk about her death—or after it, her wake. Never has a person's presence been so absent. There was no us. There were my cousins, Brian and Gerald. Her sons. They were her world. Gerald was the primary object of Anne's devotion, and being the older son, he drove the family now. A-yi-yi. He and his wife buzzed around Franny

Brown's telling each white-haired brother and sister-in-law of Tim's, each person who played Beano with Anne, each guy who worked in the uncle's drug store, all the women Anne knew from church, from Harvard where she cleaned, Gerald and Gay moved through the swaying crowd who were observing Anne lying there in her pink dress, and they quietly whispered in each aging ear, we've decided not to have anything at the house after the funeral. There was a quiet pleasure to this message: no party, nothing, go home. It was a jarring pronouncement. It divided the generations.

I began to see it at my uncle's funeral, four years before. You'd look at the heads that filled the church. You understood for the first time what a generation meant. So fragile, the white ones, dwindling, honoring one of their own, and there'd be less of them each time, all going home, not Ireland or Poland but somewhere. At Anne's they were given a shove. By my cousin who was clearly scared shitless. Without his mother, there'd be no way to gather, to put out a spread. There'd be no way to do it without her, with the feeling gone.

My mother deferred to Gerald. You've got to say something, we pleaded, but she wouldn't. It's his house, she cringed. Finally the grandchildren ran the funeral, kids in their twenties. It didn't have to be bad, but it was. The priests who said her mass knew Anne, because Anne always knew the priests. The priests stood there in their black and white vestments looking at the gang of us and the small box of Anne propped on rollers in the aisle, nice shiny wood, and the rug had some kind of modern pattern if I'm remembering correctly, the correct church. St. Raphael's in Medford. There was a black-haired priest and a white-haired one and they knew Anne. These guys almost started to cry. Anne made everyone feel like her kid. My cousin was probably jealous of the world. He needed to be alone with her in his sorrow. Then one guy got up, a boyfriend of one of my cousin's kids, a boyfriend she was trying to hold on to, so she tossed *him* the opportunity to eulogize Anne at her funeral. He said how great she was. It was the weirdest kind of insult. A room full of people, hundreds of us, her clan, and the best we can do is this vanishing boyfriend of a grandchild, a Boston deejay, who called her Mrs. D., which was the initial of her last name which was Donnellan.

My cousin Gerald was a deejay when he was a kid. So this guy was probably like him in some way. He told us who my aunt was. She was very open-minded, he pointed out. For instance, he shared, she never gave me a hard time about my ponytail. We all thought about that.

I want to get up there, I whispered to my mother. Don't you dare, she whispered back. Mom, *I speak*.

# 9.

I know that sound was first transported by Marconi. I learned it in school. It's not the same, my mother snapped when I wondered if Rosie Marcone, who made the sauce, who lived upstairs from my aunt, was related to this genius. It's not even spelled the same she said. It sounds the same, I yelled back.

May I help you, the woman asked. She was an old-style secretary. Not the kind my mother had been in the sixties, her glasses on a chain, sweet, efficient and ready to help. This woman was more like the women who were already in the office when my mother first came to work during the war. Tight perm, clean but long old teeth, tough grin. I met one of these women in a café recently in New York. She had just retired from 50 years at the *New Yorker*.

This woman was in South Wellfleet, Mass. And she had a French twist and a sweater over her shoulders. She quickly turned and asked if she could help.

She meant it, but because I said no I was gone. The woman's mind was like a beam of light that bounced against objects like me, then returned to deep work waters.

I figured I could help myself. It is the story of my life. The replica of Marconi's first machine was on a table against the right hand wall.

Piles of metal, wood, fine wood holding the entire structure of wires and bells and spools. Now I had a question. Is this Marconi's house, I asked. I wanted to know where it began, sound, the place that sends a message to the world. She was silent for a moment to acknowledge that clearly I did need help and I had stopped her again and it was unnecessary.

For years growing up, I had called my mother at work, to ask her things. There was a tone in her voice when I got her at work, she was not my mother, but my mother's secretary. She was in special time, enclosed by duty, and in its clean clothes, the day, the office held my mother just a little bit away from me. Yet she would get the message, if I spoke quickly. We were on woman's time. A woman at work. She could not stay still.

Get back on the road and keep going. That's the site. She gleamed. There's no house. I got back outside and my dog is in the driver's seat. She always is. Her triangular face and her erect ears earnestly peering at me from behind the wheel. It's exactly what we did when we were kids. Climb into the seat of power once the adult stepped out. Get back there, Rose. I pushed her ass. Brooom down the road. A sweater of deep grey was flung over everything, that was the sky, and the golden dying reeds surrounded the warm black road. Silent as only a place that was mother to sound, that received the signal. Help.

The first letter he sent was S. I don't know why, or when S became dot dash. I kissed my dog. We were standing under a stone lean-to on Cape Cod. Marconi started stringing wires immediately in his life, when he was a kid in Italy, sending messages, ten feet then fifty, a couple of miles, and eventually he sent them from right here, across the Atlantic. Would Mr. Roosevelt like to say hello to the King of England? He would. He was like their secretary but somehow just as big as them. Marconi's last invention was RCA. "His Master's Voice" became the epithet for the new revolving medium, sound, and a dog sat next to it all. That means you, Rose, and I went to hug her again.

She took off down the beach.

I believe in sound. It's the tiniest shaking, when the colors are gone, and smells disperse, the shaking continues, its effect is infinite, standing in a bowl of sand and fine reeds and wind which is something I do not understand, the lap lap lap of the water speaking to the moon, the struggling bug, nothing in the world staying still, every dropped ruler in a classroom forty years ago is a tingling moment rushing past Mars. My dog comes running and we return to the car. The click of my tooth on cement. Composers say the sounds of the orchestra playing on the Titanic can still be heard someplace at the bottom of the sea, maybe not even the very bottom, but pretty far down, and not just one spot but throughout, the tiny sound of orchestra music as some people got in the boats. There were a few, not enough, but the signal was heard.

# 10.

David sat up on his bed. Read to me, he asked. That would be very nice, and he handed me the book. Sarah Orne Jewett. His head was shaved from the treatments and there were blue chalk marks on his head so they could place the chemo where it needed to go. He looked so Iroquois. Sometimes he'd pull a stocking hat on his head and it looked odd on him, in the way Indians in movies always looked funny in white men's hats, like the clash of two cultures somebody was making a parody. I mean a pastiche. He was cold. He wrapped the covers around his body, he was in a sweater, I remember that. It was his favorite book. An old woman book, an incredible female book which told about a hopeless attraction between two women, you could watch the light flash back and forth between them. The glisten of desire. Dying is sexy. I can sit here all day, reading to you, touching my friend's cooling back. There is no place better in the world than the bedside of a friend who's dying. The landscape outside and here it was reddish vegetation and mounds of sand and rocks and stuff that looked like tumbleweed, such high value real estate can look like the desert and the wind can blow around this little house which he accidentally built in which to die. I read the story slowly and calmly. I remember the dark-haired woman, the red of her lips. The desire the women knew all their lives. That's good said David, now I have to sleep. Sometimes I'd just hold his hand. The wind whistling around the little house. I think I want to sleep now. That was very nice he said, patting the book referring to the reading. He had a headache, no a dizziness, and then the doctors opened his head and took out a big tumor and gave him a few months and we were at the end of it, David's time. He died elegant and slow. Slow in that one could see it all. It didn't happen that fast, just as slow as was predicted. First he couldn't type, and then his pen dragged across the paper awkwardly, losing control. After a while he walked crooked on the beach, and then he could only ride by the ocean in cars. His sister drove, his sister Mary, and she reminisced once about driving over this same hill in the 20's in a Model T. The ocean was glistening, full of waves, the same waves more or less at the beginning of the century, and we were in a car mounting that hill, rolling down. David, are you warm, she said. I'm fine, he smiled. There were so many small rocks in the parking lot as we pulled in. Thousands of eggs. We just sat there a while, looking at the grey sea with all the glowing light on it. It was smooth, fabulous, peaceful. We were all still alive. It was a happy day. When we first met, David would write me letters about the old women who lived in the houses of East Hampton and Amagansett when he was a boy. Odd women, like the women in books I read to him in the afternoons he was dying. They basically said the last thing that happened was the lights would go out. He would just turn off. We talked about language of course. He said it was just these marks we make on paper, like they did in Egypt on papyrus and the paper was the river. Like the oldest names in the world. These little marks tell us about the things that are coming down the river in the future. That we will be okay, that we will be fed.

# 11.

I got back to New York just in time to teach. I sat there at the head of the table as I usually do, and Jane's loft is surrounded by windows and I was talking about nature and time, which I'd like to understand. I look funny. I'm wearing a blue silk shirt and jeans. I don't usually dress this way, silk shirts are so bad. I was trying to communicate with Boston, my family, and now I look funny in New York. When they ask about my life, about living here they say "How's New York?" and it sounds like "Blue Hawk. I just stand there and think "Blue Hawk." The registration's off, it kind of saves me.

I've told this story a million times and now I'll tell it again. I grew up in the fifties. At the end of his show which was at lunch time, Big Brother Bob Emery would urge us to run into the kitchen and get our glasses of milk and "Hail to the Chief" would play on Channel 4. We sat in the den and looked at the painting of the bald President, Ike, and everyone toasted him...Bottoms up kids, all over Boston. The glass was covered in mucous and foam and our bellies felt good, full and cold.

My mother said, I'm going to go out and hang some clothes, keep an eye on your father, I don't like the way he looks. My father had been at Mass General that day. He had a brain scan. He had been having bad headaches since that fall. We would get the results, once he was dead. They looked inside him and saw nothing. Supposedly technology is better today and the tiny bleeding inside my father's brain could be read. I was just a kid and I was given an enormous job. The man on the couch was snoring. I had a pad of lined paper. Everything pours out from this one moment, a hole in my life, vast and shifting like Jupiter's eye. In school that day I was given something else—a punish task, a gift.

Due to the typical laughing and pushing that was my life when I was eleven, almost twelve, the nun, Sister Ednata, said, write 500 times "I will not talk in the corridors." The corridor to where? We were on the steps. Slate. Stone. *I will not talk. I will not talk.* Ednata gave me this gift. My father was lying on the couch. I slid open the yellowing card table. The feet of the table, wooden arcs, rested gently on the rug. I sat in the maroon chair that was his. It could have been yesterday. It's today.

The heel of my hand sliding over the paper, down the dull surface. I thought of lined paper as bars. Turn the page vertically, curl the man's hand, his fingers around the stripes of it. I see a sad face peering from behind the bars into the space of us out here—free. That's how I thought of it. I was a giant child freeing the invisible man. Around the two hundredth repetition of *I will not talk* I could see all the 'wills' crookedly lining up and the talk, talk, talk, talk, talk with the messy *k*'s. I stopped for a moment.

I was trying to decide if a public school standing I, a big capital letter, was easier than the fat loopy *I* of Ignatius Loyola which we had been taught. I even saw it in a movie. It was a big grade school screening of his life. Black and white and the sound stunk and echoed unbelievably in the auditorium. We were just all laughing, but I saw when he wrote in his diaries. I remember those big juicy *I*'s.

Yes. It would definitely go smoother and look better once my hand got crampy…and then it began. My father's blue notes. Sometimes I wake in the middle of the night and my breathing is short and I fling myself up to save me. I look around and the thing that frightens me in that wakening moment is that I am dying and I am alone. It would be the worst thing in the world to leave your life that way, and I suppose this fear is printed on my breath, breaths can suddenly go false and shallow and the bowl of you can be perched, still, and then shatter from everything that doesn't return—air, life. I took notes. I heard my father die. I saw him die, but it was the sound. I know his final notes, not the words, words are nothing. Believe me. Words are empty. It's the squawking of the animal, the wheezing, the desperate wind of a life rattling through the body, I heard him, he was not alone. This man who tried to hear me. I became possible. Now the message is complete.

I am not alone, I wrote. Words are nothing. The empty repetition of language, that holds me like a friend, a pattern, a net. I will not talk, I will not talk, my rattle, sash. I must not die alone. I heard his blue notes as he slipped away. I yelled, Mom.

Lucifer's name means light and the reason they threw him out of heaven and he became the biggest devil and not the biggest saint anymore was what he did with language. They had these words that heaven was made of, they had an order of course, a heavenly order, and Lucifer wanted to fool with it, to change the order, Lucifer was a poet. So they threw him out. The words don't matter at all. It's the sound of them, the way they come. I was sitting at the head of the table. What's first, I asked.

The windows surrounded us. Below there was a whole city of squatters, people living in tents. I look funny, I thought. Blue silk shirt. Jesus Christ. We're on Avenue D. What comes first is the title of the poem. The name. It's where you begin.

My father's name was Terrence Myles. He died in Arlington, in the state of Massachusetts, in 1961. My grandmother's name was Nellie Riordan Myles. She was born in Ireland, and she died in Massachusetts in 1957. Her body was received by the ground. I wear a blue uniform, I am sitting in school, I am flying through space in my little blue uniform. The planets go round and round. This is my record, my report, it's all I know. I'd like to thank the state of Massachusetts and the bowl of language that surrounds and survives me. My mother is still alive.